Small-Town Moms
Janet Tronstad
Debra Clopton

Love Inspired

Recycling programs
for this product may
not exist in your area.

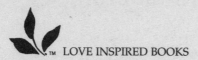

LOVE INSPIRED BOOKS

ISBN-13: 978-0-373-81539-5

SMALL-TOWN MOMS

Copyright © 2011 by Harlequin Books S.A.

The publisher acknowledges the copyright holders of the
individual works as follows:

A DRY CREEK FAMILY
Copyright © 2011 by Janet Tronstad

A MOTHER FOR MULE HOLLOW
Copyright © 2011 by Debra Clopton

www.LoveInspiredBooks.com

Printed in U.S.A.

Praise for Janet Tronstad

"An emotionally vibrant
and totally satisfying read."
—*RT Book Reviews* on *Snowbound in Dry Creek*

"Janet Tronstad presents a warm, touching story."
—*RT Book Reviews* on *At Home in Dry Creek*

"Janet Tronstad's quirky small town
and witty characters will add warmth and joy
to your holiday season."
—*RT Book Reviews* on *A Dry Creek Christmas*

Praise for Debra Clopton

"A moving romance about loss and the knowledge
that only God knows the future."
—*RT Book Reviews* on *Cowboy for Keeps*

"A touching story about accepting
that God knows what's best, even when
it's beyond human understanding."
—*RT Book Reviews* on *Her Forever Cowboy*

"Debra Clopton writes a terrific story with
a great mix of humor and tenderness."
—*RT Book Reviews* on *Dream a Little Dream*

JANET TRONSTAD

grew up on a farm in central Montana, spending many winter days reading books about the Old West and the gold rush days of Alaska. During college she got a chance to see the beauty of Alaska for herself when she worked a summer on Kodiak Island in a salmon factory, packing fish eggs for a Japanese firm. Because of those experiences, she is excited to be part of this series. Janet lives in Pasadena, California, where she writes full-time when not dreaming of other places.

DEBRA CLOPTON

was a 2004 Golden Heart finalist in the inspirational category, a 2006 Inspirational Readers' Choice Award winner, a 2007 Golden Quill winner and a finalist for the 2007 American Christian Fiction Writers Book of the Year Award. She praises the Lord each time someone votes for one of her books, and takes it as an affirmation that she is exactly where God wants her to be.

Debra is a hopeless romantic and loves to create stories with lively heroines and the strong heroes who fall in love with them. But most important, she loves showing her characters living their faith, seeking God's will in their lives one day at a time. Her goal is to give her readers an entertaining story that will make them smile, hopefully laugh and always feel God's goodness as they read her books. She has found the perfect home for her stories, writing for the Love Inspired line, and still has to pinch herself just to see if she really is awake and living her dream.

When she isn't writing, she enjoys taking road trips, reading and spending time with her two sons, Chase and Kris. She loves hearing from readers and can be reached through her website, www.debraclopton.com, or by mail at P.O. Box 1125, Madisonville, Texas 77864.

CONTENTS

A DRY CREEK FAMILY   7
Janet Tronstad

A MOTHER FOR MULE HOLLOW   157
Debra Clopton

A DRY CREEK FAMILY
Janet Tronstad

Dedicated to my sisters—Margaret Enger and Doris Tronstad. I am very grateful for you both.

And we know that all things work together for good to them that love God, to them who are called according to his purpose.

—*Romans* 8:28

Chapter One

Maegan Shay couldn't believe she'd started talking to the teddy bear. She'd been on the road for three days and her anxiety was building. If Smokey the stuffed animal hadn't been there, she'd be talking to the little brass button on her steering wheel by now. She should have waited until she arrived in Dry Creek, Montana, to make the call to the Parker family, but her first worry had been that everyone would be away from their ranch when she got to the small town. So, before she left Chicago, she phoned and told Clint Parker that she was coming to meet her nine-year-old niece.

That had been a mistake.

"He can't stop me from seeing Lilly," she turned to remind Smokey as he sat in the passenger seat of her car. She was supposed to meet her niece for the very first time when she arrived in Dry Creek. She'd already told the bear the whole story, especially the part about how the girl's uncle, Clint, had barely let her explain why she was calling before he accused her of trying to take advantage of the young girl.

"Since when is a woman in search of her family taking advantage of anyone?" she asked the bear. "If he only knew how many hours—make that *years*—I've worked to find them."

Smokey didn't answer her question, but his black button eyes did look sympathetic. He wore a sequin studded pair of suspenders and corduroy pants. She'd bought him for her niece at a gas station outside of Grand Forks when it suddenly occurred to her that Lilly might not take to strangers. Maegan hadn't at her age. Some days she still didn't, although at the age of thirty-two she could usually hide her distrust better than someone Lilly's age.

So, the bear was going to be her goodwill offering to her young niece and, by extension, to the man who appeared to be raising her. She wished she didn't feel the need for a present. She usually had more confidence. She should be a match for a rancher like Clint

Parker, even if he did have enough steel in his voice to give her visions of John Wayne holding off the bad guys. She pictured him as an older, burly man with a rifle across his knees and a scowl on his face. Not the most comforting image to have in her mind as she neared her destination, especially not when he was the one in charge of her young niece.

Maegan turned her full attention back to the road. She was used to driving in big-city traffic and it made her slightly nervous that there were no other cars in sight. The ground on both sides of the asphalt was as flat and empty as it could be. Grain fields had been cut short last fall and the stubble left to die during the winter. Plus, the sky was overcast. It was only March and spring was nowhere in sight.

She couldn't stop thinking about the phone conversation. She kept wondering if Clint would stand by his agreement to let her meet her sister's daughter. He had clearly been reluctant, like he didn't understand the importance of this trip to her.

She would think her need to see Lilly was obvious. Maegan and her sisters had been scattered across the foster care system twenty-five years ago when their parents died in a car accident. She had located her middle sister, Olivia, last fall and just recently discovered that her youngest sister, Dawn, had died three years earlier in another car crash, leaving two children behind. Each of the children were now living with their respective fathers. Olivia would be checking on the youngest child, a boy, who lived in Mule Hollow, Texas. That left Lilly for her.

Maegan glanced into the rearview mirror as she tucked her honey-colored hair behind the large amber barrette she wore. She'd learned years ago that loose hair annoyed most of the adults looking her over for adoption so she always had her barrette handy just in case she ever wanted to make a good impression. She hadn't used it much back then. She was in no hurry to be adopted. She wanted a perfect family or none at all.

Back then, she had hope. And faith. She remembered repeatedly praying to God for the perfect parents, which—in her mind—were a couple who would keep her and her sisters together. It hadn't seemed like too much to ask. She'd even found a man and woman she thought would do, but when she whispered to them about her sisters, they just shook their heads. After several of these disappointments, she finally realized no one was going to help her—not God, not the social workers, not the people who said they wanted to be parents. They all talked about families, but they didn't care about hers. Finally, she and her sisters lost track of each other.

From then on, Maegan just gave up. She had no intention of replacing her sisters or her parents with new people so she bounced around from foster home to foster home. She'd do without a family if she couldn't have the one she was born with. Almost everything else she owned had been taken away. Even her faded T-shirts were replaced with some scratchy cotton blouses that were supposed to make prospective parents like her better.

The only thing she had left was the little plastic barrette her mother had given her for her eighth birthday. That, along with her ever-changing pairs of orthopedic shoes, seemed to be the only two constants in her life. Not that she was complaining. She had long ago learned it was pointless to feel sorry for herself. A lot of other foster kids had lost everything, too.

The fact that her foot was slightly deformed, causing her to limp, might have made it harder for her to make her way than it was for others, but it had also forged in her the strength to get through law school. And the patience to cut through the endless red tape needed to find her sisters after all the paperwork mistakes that had been made in their case files over the years.

That strength was probably what had given her the courage to insist Clint Parker let her meet Lilly at the café in Dry Creek on this cold morning. It was a public place, she had told him. What harm could she do? She'd also asked him to read the packet of information she'd sent to Lilly's father, Joseph Parker, detailing the history of her and her two sisters. Apparently, Joseph was out of town, but Clint acknowledged an envelope had come for his brother. He said it was sitting unopened on top of the refrigerator in the house they shared on their family's ranch and he'd promised to read it.

Maegan slowed her car and forced her muscles to relax. She could see buildings ahead. It had to be the town of Dry Creek, even though it wasn't much to look at from a distance. The wood-frame houses had porches, but they didn't have chairs on them or hanging plants or anything that looked like it was added for beauty rather than practicality. The few trees around had no leaves, just those long gray branches reaching upward to nowhere.

As she got closer, she saw that many of the houses needed a new coat of paint or, at least, a good hosing down to remove the traces of dried mud from their clapboard sides. It must have been a hard winter. The only building that gleamed with cleanliness was a church with a short steeple; the white paint on its walls reflected what little sun came through the clouds until the place practically shone.

She, of course, already knew God didn't have much to do with foster kids like her, but she didn't begrudge others their faith. Life was always a little rougher and muddier for strays like her; it was just the way it was. She did wonder though what made people shine up their house of worship before they painted their own houses. God must answer a lot of their prayers for them to be that pleased with Him.

She slowed her car more. There were no sidewalks in this town and no formal parking spaces, either. The sign leading into town said one hundred sixty-seven people lived here, but she thought that might be an exaggeration. As she looked around, everything looked worn. Even the two-lane asphalt road that went through the town was caked with brown dirt. A couple of pickup trucks were parked in front of a hardware store and another car was sitting farther down the road.

She didn't care about the hardware store so she studied the café instead. White ruffled curtains hung in the windows and a large porch led to the front door. She couldn't see into the café, but a light was on inside so it had to be open. She pulled off the road next to the black pickup and stopped. For good or bad, she had arrived.

Clint Parker watched Lilly crumble the piece of toast that was left on her breakfast plate. She was one forlorn little girl. They were sitting at a table in the café, waiting to meet the woman who claimed to be her aunt. For the life of him, he didn't know why he'd agreed to let a stranger talk to Lilly. The woman could have said she was the Queen of Sheba and how was he to know if she really was or not?

"Remember, you don't need to tell this woman anything about yourself," Clint reminded his niece. He'd almost taken Lilly over to her Sunday school teacher's house so she would be somewhere safe while he figured out if this woman was legitimate.

Lilly shrugged, but didn't look up to meet his eyes.

The two of them had enough trouble without some woman coming around stirring up painful memories. Lilly didn't talk about her dead mother; he wasn't sure what she would say to someone claiming to be her mother's very alive sister. As far as he knew, there had been no mention of an aunt when Lilly was delivered to his brother last fall.

It had taken social services a few years to track down his brother since Joe had been sweet-talked into going down to Brazil and working for some rodeo organization there. Clint suspected there had been a woman involved, but his brother never said and he never asked. He wished now that he had urged his brother to come home sooner. Lilly spent those years bouncing around to various foster families and it hadn't done her any good. Eventually, Joe came back and voted in Montana for the first time in years. That let everyone know where he was.

Clint realized he should have asked Maegan Shay to send some identification when he talked to her on the phone. Of course, he had read the packet of information she had sent, but what did that prove? With digital photo programs, anyone with a computer could have created some of those forms.

Clint looked down at his niece. "I'll ask Linda to bring you some ice cream before we go back home."

The Engers owned this café and, although Linda was back in the kitchen at the moment, he knew she'd check with him soon. She'd stocked up on maple nut ice cream when he found out it was Lilly's favorite. Not that ice cream did enough to make his niece happy. He was at his wit's end. A girl her age should chatter away and laugh and—he stopped himself. He honestly had no idea how a nine-year-old girl should act. All he knew was that she should make some kind of noise.

Lilly was the quietest little thing he'd ever seen. He had been on his knees every night for the past three months, asking God to show him how to make her happy. That's how long ago Joe had left her with him, saying she slowed him down on the rodeo circuit. *Slowed him down?* She'd only been with him two months. Clint had almost given his brother a tongue-lashing for even thinking his daughter could be a bother—and having the nerve to say so in front of her—but then Clint had looked down and his heart squeezed tight. Lilly's shoulders were soldier straight. Her small face was stoic and her eyes focused on her feet. At first, he thought there was something wrong with her shoes and then he saw they were orthopedic ones.

Joe had seen him looking and nodded wearily. So, the feet were the deal-breaker with his brother. It was obvious Lilly had some kind of problem and couldn't walk fast enough to please him. That sounded like Joe. He was never willing to stay through the hard times with anyone.

Clint hadn't known what to say to his brother or his niece so he'd announced that, of course, Lilly should stay on the ranch with him. It was her home. He added that he could use some company, although that wasn't strictly true. He'd almost become a recluse over the past few years since his father had died, not even going to church regularly. Clint's failing was the opposite of Joe's. He stayed with things too long. If there was a lost cause out there, he'd sign up for it. Knowing that, he kept himself apart from what he called complications. Mostly, that meant people and the emotions they brought with them.

Clint had been engaged briefly five or six years ago to a woman he'd met on a cruise sponsored by the cattleman's association. As eager as a lovesick pup, he'd proposed to the woman in the Caribbean moonlight. She had ended the relationship a month later, saying she could not live on the ranch with him. It had broken his heart. He suffered for a time until he realized his engagement had taught him a valuable lesson. He just wasn't good with people. His mother died when he was young, but he could tell she had been often disappointed with his father. Clint figured he was the same, letting people down in some way he didn't even understand. Since then he'd thought twice before he committed to anyone, even a helpless little girl.

Still, Lilly had stood there looking lost and he didn't trust Joe not to send her back to the social services agency. He didn't know what would happen then. Clint couldn't have that on his conscience, or on his heart. He had to risk taking her in.

Of course, he'd had no idea how hard it would be for him and Lilly to connect. They often sat silent in the house together. He made sure he fed her well, but she didn't seem to have much of an appetite. Or anything she wanted to say. Maybe that's why he'd agreed to this meeting. He'd try almost anything to see her happier.

"Mrs. Hargrove said she had some more beads for you," Clint added as they sat there. The older woman was Lilly's Sunday school teacher. She was a big help to him, even coming out to the ranch house to give him a few lessons so he could make some of the food Lilly liked. He couldn't expect the girl to thrive on steaks and fried potatoes, which was his usual fare when he was by himself. The older woman was the one who suggested Lilly needed a hobby.

It was the only idea Lilly had grasped with enthusiasm. Now, she was intent on decorating a horse bridle for Joe's birthday. She would sit for hours at the kitchen table with her tongue caught between her front teeth as she concentrated on pushing a needle through the cheap vinyl bridle she'd found in the barn. Clint had suggested she use one of the nicer leather ones until he saw she didn't have the strength to push the needle through any of them. He had already told Joe in no uncertain terms he was to be home a week from next Wednesday, regardless of what rodeo his new lady-of-the-month wanted him to enter. The way Joe was moving from woman to woman made Clint wonder if his brother hadn't had his heart broken in Brazil before he came back. Neither of the Parker brothers was very good at love. Their father had seen to that.

"We'll head on over to Mrs. Hargrove's place if the woman doesn't get here soon," Clint said. He had enough to worry about for himself and Lilly; Joe would have to take care of himself. "Then we'll come back for ice cream afterward. How does that sound?"

Lilly shrugged.

Clint figured he would wait another five minutes for the woman and not a second longer. Just then he heard the door to the café open.

The minute Clint had looked up he'd known it was Maegan Shay. How did she manage to look so fragile? Maybe it was the teddy bear she held that made her seem young. No, it was her skin that did it. The door was open behind her and the morning light made her skin seem translucent. Pale freckles were sprinkled across her nose. Strands of blond hair swept back from her face in a loose style of some sort. Her eyes were solemn and large. She seemed hesitant.

"You can't be an attorney," he blurted out

when she took a step closer. The paperwork had said she was thirty-two, but she didn't look more than nineteen.

A pink blush swept over her face. "I passed the bar exam so technically I am—even though I'm working as a paralegal now. The firm has promised me the next opening though. They like my work."

Clint was pulled back by the quiet dignity of her words. "I'm sorry. It's none of my business."

He stood up and waited for her to arrive at their table before arranging a chair for her.

"We don't have much time," he added as she sat down. He actually had all morning, but somehow he didn't think he should spend too much time in the presence of this woman. She reminded him of a butterfly and he half expected her to flit away. He didn't want to risk disappointing Lilly if she did.

"I appreciate you seeing me on such short notice," she said.

Clint grunted as she sat down. She might look like a butterfly, but she had that same stiff way of moving that Lilly did—like she wasn't sure if she was welcome. For the first time he believed she really was Lilly's aunt. He was going to ask if she'd like him to call for some more coffee when he saw that she wasn't listening to him. All of her attention had moved to Lilly.

Suddenly, he realized all of the reasons a genuine relative might want to see Lilly.

"Joe—he wins some at the rodeos, but he doesn't have much in the way of steady money. He probably does owe back child support to Lilly's mother though. Well, her estate I guess now. I'm sure there were expenses with everything. If that's what you need, we can come to some agreement." Joe wouldn't pay anything, but Clint figured he could spare ten or twenty thousand dollars. The crops had been good last year. And he believed in paying his family's debts.

"I don't want any money."

Clint saw distaste twist the woman's mouth, but he couldn't even speak his worst fear.

Dear Lord, don't let her be here for Lilly. I know Joe is her father, but if someone challenged it, the courts might not see the wisdom of him raising her. I'm not even sure I see the wisdom of him raising her. But she's a Parker. She needs to be with her family—even if it's just me.

Clint took a deep breath. The woman didn't seem interested in talking to him and he wasn't going to give voice to his fears anyway so he kept quiet. No point in arming the enemy.

"I brought you a present." Maegan held out the teddy bear to the girl.

Clint figured Lilly would ignore the bear. He'd already bought her stuffed animals and a funny-looking raccoon puppet. She hadn't shown any interest in anything resembling a toy. She had several tiny porcelain dolls that she kept locked away in her suitcase, but he figured they were more like keepsakes than toys. Then he saw a tiny flicker in the middle of the brown fur and saw that the suspenders the bear was wearing were studded with brass beads of some sort. And it looked like red glass beads lined the animal's collar.

"I'm making a bridle," Lilly said as she reached for the bear.

"Well, that's good," the woman said as she smiled down at the child. "Do you have a horse?"

As he expected, Lilly shook her head as she folded herself back into her silence. The brown bear was big enough she could almost hide behind it. She shifted it in her arms and there was the sound of something dropping to the floor of the café. One of the shiny brass beads from the suspenders had fallen off and rolled away from the table.

"I'll get it," Lilly said as she stood up and took a few steps toward it.

Clint saw the woman freeze when she saw Lilly's limp and then her shoes. He had been trying to find some kind of shoes that would be comfortable for Lilly but wouldn't label her as a girl with problem feet. She had brachymetatarsia which meant one toe was shorter than it should be. She could have an operation to correct it when her feet were fully grown, but for now she had to wear special shoes and walk as best she could. There was nothing really wrong with Lilly though and he didn't want some big-city woman looking down her nose at her. Not every little girl was tiptoeing around in play high heels, dreaming of being a princess, and he dared anyone to pity his niece.

"Lilly likes beads," Clint said, more for the sake of distracting the woman than for telling her anything she couldn't see for herself.

The woman nodded and glanced over at Clint. At least that meant she wasn't staring at Lilly.

"She's making the bridle for her father. My brother, Joe," Clint added.

"Yes." The woman brought her gaze back to him. She was allowing Lilly to walk back to the table unobserved. "He's away at a rodeo, I think you said earlier."

Clint nodded. He had to admit she was sensitive to Lilly's feelings. He didn't want to talk about Joe, but, if he had to say something, he wanted to make his brother look as good as possible—which was hard because he hadn't seen his brother since he brought Lilly to the ranch. "He's never more than a phone call away."

Well, of course, except for when he was in Brazil, Clint thought, realizing too late he'd left himself wide open. She must know his brother had been unreachable for years. That was part of Lilly's foster care system record.

"Lilly loves her father," he added quickly and forced himself to smile. "He should be back in a week or so."

The woman nodded. "Good. I'd like to meet him."

"But—" Clint sputtered. He never would have said anything if he thought there was a chance she'd want to stay and meet Joe. "His rodeo schedule is pretty much up in the air.

And we wouldn't want to keep you. He might not get back for a while."

"But his birthday—" Lilly interrupted, panic in her voice.

"Oh, I'm sure he'll be back for his birthday." Clint regretted his earlier words already. "But that's not until the week after next. Miss Shay, here, has to get back to her job."

"I have time." With that, the woman folded her hands and leaned back in her chair.

"But Dry Creek doesn't have a hotel," Clint protested with the first reason that came to mind. A beautiful woman like her would want a million nice things that this small town didn't offer. He knew that because his ex-fiancée had taken one look at Dry Creek and dumped him rather than attempt to spend a lifetime here. A woman like the one in front of him probably felt the same need for beauty salons and gourmet restaurants. Of course, it wasn't like she was deciding to spend her life here. Even his ex-fiancée could have managed a few days if she'd tried.

The woman shrugged. "I'll find someplace to stay. It doesn't need to be fancy."

Clint was trying to think of more reasons to convince her to leave. But then Lilly spoke.

"Did you know my mother? Before she went to heaven?"

"No, sweetie," the woman said softly. "But I knew her mother, your grandmother."

All of Clint's resolve left him. The woman might be able to give some comfort to Lilly. Maybe she could get Lilly to chatter away like a little girl should. Lilly certainly had never responded to him when he asked about her mother.

Clint swallowed and said what he needed to say. "Mrs. Hargrove-Nelson—well, I always still think of her as Mrs. Hargrove—has a room over her garage that she sometimes rents out for a few days. She's got the first house on your left as you drive into town. I'll see Lilly has time to visit with you if you stay. You can tell Mrs. Hargrove I sent you."

"Is hers the house with the picket fence around it?"

Clint nodded. "That's the one."

His fate was sealed. But he was willing to suffer more than the company of one unknown woman if it would make Lilly happy. The truth was he and Lilly needed help. The woman probably even knew how to braid hair. Clint had braided a horse tail or two in his time and he'd made the mistake of thinking that braiding a little girl's hair would be the same. Lilly had been in tears yesterday when she looked in the mirror. Her mother apparently had always started the braid higher on the back of her head.

Clint never thought he'd be a father, especially not to a girl. He might have managed to guide a boy into manhood, but Lilly needed things he didn't even know about. His need had driven him back to church, and he'd been praying more than he had in his life since Lilly came. But things hadn't improved much. Maybe he needed to be open to the possibility that God was answering his prayer with this woman. *Just don't let her take Lilly from me. I'll do anything else You ask, Lord. Just, please, not that.*

Chapter Two

Maegan woke the next morning and squinted as she lay in bed. Bright sunlight was streaming in the window and hitting the wall above her head. She'd had her doubts yesterday, but the room over Mrs. Hargrove's garage was lovely. A small bathroom was off to one side, and the main room held a double bed covered with white cotton bedding and the softest pillows Maegan had ever known. She wondered idly if the older woman had made the pillows from the feathers of some geese she'd had on the farm where she'd lived before retiring and moving into Dry Creek. In the short time she'd spent with Mrs. Hargrove yesterday, Maegan had learned the older woman had all kinds of "country" skills.

Maegan stretched. She had slept deeply, but was still surprised to awake feeling so content. She wondered if it was because she had found another piece of the mosaic that was her family. She never pictured herself as a wife or mother. All of her hope of belonging to a family had gone when God didn't provide her with adoptive parents willing to take her and her two sisters. Maybe that's why finding her birth family, even though it was too late to be a family in the same way, was so satisfying.

She'd called her sister Olivia last night before going to bed. Her sister said she'd been waiting to hear all about their niece. Olivia had a daughter about Lilly's age and she said that, from what she had heard, Lilly seemed to be doing well enough for her age.

Maegan felt a little guilty because she didn't mention Lilly's foot problem. Maybe it was because watching the girl had been like looking into the mirror of her past. She had known her foot problem, brachymetatarsia, was inherited, but it was still rare enough she had never expected anyone else in the family to suffer with it.

Besides, there was no need for Olivia to worry about Lilly. She had enough problems just getting her and her daughter ready to make their trip to Mule Hollow to visit Lilly's younger brother.

Maegan wanted to be the one to worry about Lilly. The girl needed an aunt who understood what it was like to feel clumsy and misshapen. Maegan knew she wasn't suited to being a mother, but helping Lilly with her foot problems was close to parenting. She was surprised that she relished the prospect. In fact, if it ever worked out for Lilly to come live with her, she would—

Whoa—that thought stopped her cold and made her sit up in bed. Where had that idea come from? She hadn't driven to Dry Creek intending to do anything crazy like ask Lilly to live with her. She had only wanted to be sure the girl was all right, that she had someone to care for her. Maegan knew she had no business trying to raise a child. Parenting was a mystery to her; she had known so little of it herself she didn't even know all of the mistakes she could make.

Unfortunately, once she tasted the idea, it rolled around in her mind like some out-of-control marble. It was a foolish thing to think about on a morning like this, but she couldn't seem to let it go.

She swung her legs over the side of the bed, shaking her head just to get some blood moving through it. She had done enough research when challenging the foster care system in her search for her sisters that she knew how important good parenting was. So many things could go wrong. She would do better to spend her time looking at the realities that were in place now instead of daydreaming that she would make a good mother. Lilly might not trust Clint, but he cared about her. It was obvious when he looked at the girl. Lilly probably just needed more time to adjust to the changes in her life. She'd gone from living with her mother, to living with her rodeo-loving father, to staying on the ranch with—

Maegan stopped herself again. It hadn't really sunk in until now that Clint wasn't Lilly's guardian any more than she was. The person who should be here taking care of Lilly was her father. He was supposed to be the pillar in her life. Where was the man? How many rodeos did the man ride in anyway? What if he took it into his mind to go back to Brazil?

She stood up on the cold wood floor and wished she had socks on her feet. Even with the morning sunshine, she wouldn't mind some additional warmth. She'd do well to find out more about both of the Parker brothers.

There was a knock at the door and a voice called out. "It's Edith."

Mrs. Hargrove-Nelson had instructed her

yesterday to call her by her first name even though Maegan didn't feel right doing so. Instead, she followed the lead of others and called her Mrs. Hargrove. According to Clint, the older woman had become so well-known in this community that most people still called her what they had for years even after she married her long-time friend, Charlie Nelson. She didn't seem to mind and neither did he.

"Come in," Maegan invited as she combed her fingers through her hair. Her barrette was on the top of the dresser, but it would take too long to pull her hair back.

The older woman opened the door and peeked around it. Smile lines crowded her plain face and her eyes were warm. Her gray hair was set in pin curls and covered with a black net. She stepped into the room and Maegan saw she wore a loose-fitting gingham housedress, covered by a white bib apron, and black sensible shoes with ties and thick heels. She held a small tray that looked a little heavy.

"Remember, the room comes with my complimentary breakfast," the older woman said.

Maegan walked over to take the tray. "It smells wonderful, but you shouldn't have carried it up the stairs. I would have gladly gone down and brought it up."

"I can manage," the woman said with a grin as she handed over the tray. "Besides, my Charlie fixed those steps last spring so they're a pure pleasure to climb."

A plate with two biscuits sat on the tray next to a silver butter knife and a small jar of melted honey. A delicate china cup was sitting next to a dish of butter. A red thermos stuck out of Mrs. Hargrove's apron pocket and, now that Maegan had taken the tray from her, the older woman set it on the dresser.

"This looks delicious." Maegan carefully set the tray down on the dresser as well. She had bought some twist-it cans of biscuits over the years. But these biscuits made those look like rocks. Golden brown and fluffy, they were just right. Who made biscuits like these anymore?

A mother, that's who, Maegan realized. A woman who believed in making the food her family ate with her own hands. A woman like that probably canned her own fruit and pinned her laundry on an outside line to dry in the summer sun.

"Do you knit?" Maegan asked, suddenly feeling the weight of her inadequacies. She didn't know how to do any of those things. She'd make a terrible mother.

"I can knit a little." Mrs. Hargrove looked up in surprise. "Mostly just the basic stitches though."

"You daughter must have loved that." Maegan had already heard about the older woman's grown daughter. Apparently, Doris June had returned to Dry Creek some years ago and married her old high school sweetheart. "With the knitting and the biscuits, what girl wouldn't love it?"

Mrs. Hargrove smiled. "Well, mine wasn't too excited about my knitting when she was growing up, but she used to love my biscuits. Until she became a teenager. Then, she worried there were too many calories. But once in a while on a Sunday morning she'd have one and—oh, her face, it just lit up with happiness."

Mrs. Hargrove looked as though she were remembering those days. Then she brought herself back. "Well, you don't want to hear about all that. I forgot to mention I serve breakfast early on Sunday mornings. I always get up around six so I can go over my lesson—I teach a Sunday school class."

"You really must have been a great mother." The woman was even a teacher.

Mrs. Hargrove shook her head. "I made some big mistakes. Most parents do, I suppose, but I have to think my prayers were what made the difference."

Maegan didn't know what to say. She wasn't surprised that God would answer the prayers of a sweet old lady like Mrs. Hargrove. "That's nice." She felt something more was required in the conversation, but it took her a minute. "I suppose you know all about how to pray."

Maegan had always been curious about those people who got answers to their prayers. She wondered if she had made some mistake in the way she prayed as a child. She'd tried really hard back then to convince God that it was important for her and her sisters to be together, but maybe she'd folded her hands wrong or called Him by the wrong name or something.

Maybe God just didn't like her. Whatever the reason He hadn't wanted to help her, she figured it was best left unspoken.

The aroma of brewed tea spread throughout the room as Maegan opened the thermos. The older woman had asked last night if she preferred coffee or tea.

"There's no special know-how in praying to God," Mrs. Hargrove said quietly. "He's the one who does the work. We just talk to Him."

"Oh." Maegan swallowed and forgot about the tea she'd just poured. She had held out hope that she had made a mistake all those years ago that could be corrected. Now, it seemed His indifference was personal. "He didn't do anything when I prayed to Him."

"When was that, dear?"

"A long time ago—" Maegan stopped. "It doesn't matter anymore."

"Of course, it does," Mrs. Hargrove said as she stepped closer and put her hand on Maegan's arm. "Especially if you still remember it."

"I'm not likely to forget."

Maegan started to lift her cup of tea before setting it back down and blurting out, "I don't think He wanted me to pray."

"God wants everyone to have the kind of relationship with Him that makes them want to visit with Him in prayer," the older woman stated with quiet confidence.

"Visit?" Maegan was taken back. "I hadn't planned on visiting. I just asked Him for something."

Mrs. Hargrove nodded. "Like throwing a coin in a wishing well?"

"I suppose."

"Well, that is the problem right there. God isn't a wishing well."

It was silent for a moment, then the older woman spoke. "Lilly's in my Sunday school class this morning. I thought you might like to sit in today so you can be with her."

Maegan forgot all about God as she thought about the invitation. This might be her only opportunity to see how her niece acted around other children. The girl had seemed so subdued yesterday and the time they'd spent together at the café had been short. Surely with her friends she would be more animated.

Still, Maegan didn't want to make anyone uncomfortable. "Have you asked Clint about that? He seems to keep a close eye on Lilly. I know he's said I can see her, but I don't think he'd want me to just show up someplace where she is. You know, without warning or anything."

Mrs. Hargrove smiled. "He loves his niece. But he'd agree everyone is welcome at the church."

"I hope you're right."

The smile left Mrs. Hargrove's face and she was serious. "Clint might not always come across as the most friendly man you'll ever meet, but there's not a man around with a better heart. He grew up hard, with a father who wasn't much good for anything. Raised his younger brother, too. And he'd lay down his life for Lilly if he had to——"

Maegan gave a curt nod. She knew she shouldn't say anything to anyone, but she had never been too successful at holding her tongue. Besides, she didn't have time to be subtle. "Clint's not really the one with custody though, is he?"

Mrs. Hargrove's face went a little pale. "It would break Clint's heart if you took that girl away from here."

"But how about Lilly's father?" Maegan pressed on. "How does he feel about being with her?"

Mrs. Hargrove pressed her lips together. "Joe is still finding his way in life. But he means well—he's just——"

The other woman didn't need to say any more. Maegan could write a book about parents who meant well. The foster care system was full of stories like that. She looked at Mrs. Hargrove. "I think I'll take you up on your invitation. I'd enjoy getting to know Lilly better."

Mrs. Hargrove nodded. "We're going to be

talking about King Solomon today. Do you have a Bible with you?"

"Me? No." She didn't own a Bible. After her prayer incident, she had avoided everything to do with church. Some years later, after she was on her own, she had looked up the Christmas story one December when she was in a hotel room in Milwaukee. She'd read it straight through, but hadn't believed much of what she read. God really wouldn't send a baby some place where the little one might be killed, would He? No wonder He hadn't answered her prayer. Child Protective Services would be all over someone who did that today. Hopefully this King Solomon would know better than to endanger a baby.

"I'll be happy to lend you one of my Bibles for the day then," Mrs. Hargrove said. "It helps to read the story for yourself."

Maegan was going to take the older woman's word for it. She didn't have time to start reading the Bible. She had to figure out what Lilly's future should be. One thing she knew for sure, she wasn't going to soften and say that Joe Parker was suited to being a parent for her niece unless she knew it was one hundred percent true.

Now that she had met Lilly, she wanted to make sure the girl had the best life possible.

Maegan hadn't found the perfect family for herself when she was growing up, but she'd find it for Lilly if she had to. It was one of the reasons she'd taken the loans to become a lawyer. She wanted to be able to help her family, financially and in other ways, and she'd realized the law helped her to do that.

Clint felt like he'd been squeezed into the shape of a pretzel and then stomped upon until he was low to the ground. He was sitting on a child's wooden chair in the church basement. Small square windows lined the top of the concrete room and a row of crayon pictures of Moses parting the Red Sea were taped midway between the windows and the gray speckled linoleum floor. Mrs. Hargrove's Sunday school class was supposed to be for eight- and nine-year-olds, but the woman was so beloved there were kids as old as fifteen mixed in with the regular attendees. Clint's only excuse for being there was that Mrs. Hargrove had called and told him Maegan was going to sit in for the class.

He wasn't surprised the woman would take an opportunity like this to be with Lilly, but he was astonished Mrs. Hargrove had called. She was usually too busy before church to do anything. And, when he got off the phone, he realized she had been trying to tell him something without saying it directly.

He figured Mrs. Hargrove didn't have any hard and cold facts or she would have told him up front what she was thinking. But, if she was uneasy about Maegan being in the class, Clint wasn't going to ignore her intuition. Mrs. Hargrove was the wisest person he knew. So he went to the children's class when he got to the church instead of staying upstairs with the adults.

Lilly hadn't seemed to care if he was there or not.

He glanced across the table and saw Maegan huddled next to the girl. He studied the woman even though he didn't know what he was looking for. She looked more like a lawyer today than she had yesterday. She wore a maroon pantsuit with a black scarf tied around her neck. She wore no jewelry. Her skin was paler than it had been yesterday, but probably only because the light down here was mostly from the florescent bulbs overhead and they tended to bleach the color out of everything. Maegan was serious though, no question about it.

And then something in him shifted and he saw the subtle beauty of her face. She was leaning over to look at something Lilly had in her hand and he saw the woman's neck had the sculpted sweep of a Greek goddess statue. All cool ivory. Her lips were tilted up at the corners in a tiny smile that would rival the Mona Lisa's. He hadn't noticed before that she was a work of art. He pulled his gaze away from her before someone caught him staring. He had no business being taken with her.

There wasn't a parade of single women going through Dry Creek, but there were enough that, even if he decided he wanted to date, he didn't need to be attracted to this woman. When he saw her, he should see a big red X in front of his eyes. She would be trouble even without Lilly in the picture. Not that it made any difference what he thought. He didn't have a chance with her in the romance department. She wanted to see Lilly and that's why she was here.

Suddenly, he realized Maegan hadn't looked him in the eyes this morning. Not once. Yesterday, her eyes had alternately stormed at him and accused him. Today she wasn't letting him in.

He probably should be worried, but it was hard to think that someone in a child's chair was a serious threat to his family. And, he had to admit she was being a good sport about everything. She had apparently been well pleased with her room over Mrs. Hargrove's garage. It looked like she wasn't as much like his ex-fiancée as he had thought.

He should have known Maegan was different after he sat down last night and reread those papers she had sent—the ones that were copies of the foster care records. He hadn't bothered to put the pieces together earlier, but last night he thought about what the notations on the pages meant. Family after family had passed over Maegan for adoption. He'd seen the report of a doctor's visit. She had the same foot problem as Lilly. The records said she was stubborn and refused to make herself suitable for adoption. She had told one social worker she was waiting for the right family and then refused to explain what she had meant. For another, she refused to stand still so her limp would not be noticed. Clint had felt like cheering for her as he sat there.

She clearly gave as good as she got even back then.

Just knowing those things about her was changing his opinion of her. He no longer thought of her as some distant relative who might try to interfere with Lilly's life. The truth was he was starting to like Maegan. And to respect her. And to wish there was some way he could give her what she wanted.

Looking at her and Lilly together softened him. They looked enough alike to be mother and daughter. It wasn't so much that their coloring was the same or anything to do with their bone structure. It was their movements and the angle at which they held their heads that was the same. What if they were meant to be together? Not full-time, of course. Lilly belonged on the ranch with him. But maybe Maegan could visit over the holidays. Or maybe Lilly could fly to Chicago for a couple of weeks in the summer to be with Maegan. People worked these things out, he told himself. He had no reason to worry.

Chapter Three

The class was making gold crowns for King Solomon so Maegan was helping Lilly cut the triangles she needed to put together the cardboard headpiece. Mrs. Hargrove was talking about King Solomon at the same time and Maegan was partially listening to her as she made cuts with the scissors. She didn't miss the fact that two women had come to the king both claiming they were the rightful mother of the same child. She supposed Mrs. Hargrove was going to give some platitudes that would speak to her and Clint.

But that's not what happened. Mrs. Hargrove reported that King Solomon suggested cutting the child in half. With a sword or knife or something awful.

"That's outrageous," Maegan protested

softly as soon as she recovered from the shock of what the man had proposed thousands of years ago. She was vaguely aware that the children had all turned to look at her with wide eyes. "I mean, no one would do that today. And, if they did, the state's child custody services would stop them. Surely, even back then, they had some laws. Where were all those judges and prophets people talk about?"

Maegan ended up looking across the table toward Clint for help. She didn't know why she turned to him. He was tall and strong, but there was nothing he could do about what had happened so long ago. She didn't expect him to respond to her, but he reached across the table and put his hand over hers. Her pride told her she should move her hand, but his large calloused hand covering hers made her feel secure.

"No one hurt the child," he whispered. "It's okay."

Maegan felt the flush creep up her neck. She didn't like feeling foolish. But when she looked up into Clint's eyes she didn't see any hint that he thought she'd been silly. If anything, he looked concerned. It was the first time she'd looked at him and found this kind of caring.

"I didn't know," Maegan finally whispered back.

The silence around them suddenly made her realize that they had an audience. A dozen children were staring at them. Even Lilly's eyes were wide. Maegan looked down the table at Mrs. Hargrove. "Sorry."

"Don't be," the older woman said and smiled. She looked very pleased. "Sometimes when I tell one of these stories, it's like it's happening right in front of me, too. Time doesn't seem to matter. God likes us to be carried away as we hear about what happened."

The explanation seemed to make the children relax.

"They're holding hands," one little girl finally said with a giggle as she pointed at where Clint's hands covered Maegan's. "And in Sunday school."

"That's perfectly all right," Mrs. Hargrove said in a voice that suddenly made it normal. "We hold hands sometimes, too, when we pray."

"Not like that," the girl continued. "My mother says if you hold a boy's hand that means you like him."

"Well, we're supposed to like everyone, aren't we?" Mrs. Hargrove told the girl gently. "And since you seem to be interested in boy-friends, can you guess how many wives King Solomon had? It's more than you'd think."

The children were distracted and Maegan slipped her hand out from under Clint's. It wasn't just that it gave the children the wrong idea. She wanted to be sure she didn't have the wrong idea, either. She and Clint were just—well, not friends. Maybe one could say they were friendly. For the moment anyway.

Mrs. Hargrove finished the story and Maegan noted to herself that she didn't understand King Solomon or God or men in general.

"What's wrong?" Clint asked quietly. As everyone had been finishing up their crowns, he had walked around the table so he was sitting next to her and Lilly.

"I picked the wrong mother," she said.

Clint raised an eyebrow in question.

Maegan looked at him and saw that he seemed to care what she thought so she told him. "It's just that everyone wants the real mother to have her baby back. That's okay. But what about the other woman? Maybe she couldn't have a baby of her own. Maybe she prayed to God to make her a mother. Maybe no one even listened to her when she said she wanted a family. Maybe God didn't answer her prayer."

Maegan knew her face was flushed. But she couldn't help it. She was serious. "Maybe she felt she had no other choice."

Clint looked at her without saying anything for a while. The children were putting away their scissors and colored paper. Lilly had stood up and gone over to the bin to return some markers with two of the other girls. Mrs. Hargrove was at the end of the table gathering up papers. The sounds of children moving were all around them.

Maegan felt an urge to go return something to a box somewhere, too. She felt uncomfortable as Clint kept looking at her. Finally, she lowered her eyes to the floor.

"You're going to ask for full custody of Lilly, aren't you?" Clint asked, his voice tightly controlled.

Maegan looked over at him. He sat in the little chair and his shoulders were hunched over. He had a sprinkling of gold glitter on his hair and a streak of blue marker on his face. He'd left his Stetson on the top shelf and his sleeve had a wet stain on it where one of the boys had spilled his fruit juice. He'd clearly enjoyed making the crowns. No doubt he deserved to be a father, too.

She breathed out and felt miserable. "I don't know. I—"

Clint held up his hand as Lilly walked back toward them. "We'll talk later."

Maegan nodded as Lilly came over and stood in front of her.

"I put the scissors away," the girl announced proudly.

"That's good," Maegan murmured as she put her hand on the girl's arm.

Lilly gave her a tentative smile that was sweet and shy. "My mama always told me to put the scissors away when I was done."

Maegan blinked and forced herself to stay calm. "You must miss your mama."

Lilly nodded and gave Maegan a quick hug before turning away and walking back to join the other children.

Maegan watched her go before she looked over at Clint. His face had become drawn and grim.

"She's had enough loss in her life," Maegan said quietly. "I don't intend to try and take your place with her."

"Maybe you should," Clint said. "She means the world to me, but maybe you should be the one to raise her."

Then he stood up and walked right out of the room.

Maegan wished she could call him back, but she didn't know what she could say. Was he really suggesting that she should be Lilly's parent? She looked down at her folded hands as she listened to the sounds of his boots hitting the stairs as he made his way to the top.

When she looked up, all of the children had left the room. It was only her and Mrs. Hargrove sitting at the table.

"He doesn't know me very well." Maegan looked straight ahead at the older woman. It was clear that Mrs. Hargrove had heard what Clint had said. "I'm not sure I'd be a very good mother. I wouldn't know anything about raising a child. She's probably better off with Clint. I mean, she clearly adores her father. His brother. And when would she see Joe if she was in Chicago? And Clint would do anything for her."

Mrs. Hargrove's eyes softened as Maegan spoke. "It's in your heart though, isn't it? The desire to mother Lilly?"

Maegan nodded. "Of course. She's special. I want her to have the best. Much better than I ever had."

"So does Clint," the older woman said.

With that, Mrs. Hargrove stood up and started walking toward the stairs. "I suggest we all pray about it."

Maegan grunted as she followed the other woman toward the stairs.

Mrs. Hargrove turned around to put her hand on one of Maegan's arms. "I know you don't think He listens to you. But you just don't know Him well enough yet to trust that He will answer."

Maegan didn't know what to say to that so she nodded. That seemed to satisfy Mrs. Hargrove and the two women walked up the stairs together.

When they stepped into the small hallway at the top of the stairs, the first thing Maegan noticed was that the whole day was gray. The windows here didn't offer any more light than the ones below. She hoped she could slip through the kitchen and get outside before the church service began. She wanted to go someplace quiet and think about prayer and Lilly and what Clint had said.

She followed Mrs. Hargrove into the deserted kitchen.

Then Mrs. Hargrove turned and patted her arm as though she understood Maegan's reluctance to stay and was giving a blessing on whichever decision she made.

"Come over for dinner," the older woman offered as they stood there. "I have a chicken noodle casserole in the oven. It's enough to feed an army."

"Oh, I couldn't impose—you have your family and—" Maegan looked around at the old worn counters as though she could find a reason written there to refuse a perfectly kind invitation. She wasn't used to people being so thoughtful and it made her feel awkward.

"It's just Charlie and I today—Doris June and her family were going to come, but Ben has a bad cold so they're staying home. We'd love to have you join us."

Clint stepped back into the kitchen. He'd been out in the foyer talking crops with some of the other men when he'd heard Maegan's voice. Something about it made him think she was in trouble. It was unlikely to be true, but he excused himself anyway.

When he saw her, she had her head bent and was listening to Mrs. Hargrove.

The older woman looked up and saw him. "Come help me convince Maegan here to come to dinner after church."

"I thought I'd just get something at the café," Maegan said as she turned to him. "I don't want to be any trouble."

Clint smiled. "Only one thing wrong with that plan. The café is closed on Sundays."

"Oh."

"And you won't get a better dinner in the whole county than what you'll find at Mrs. Hargrove's table."

The older woman turned to Clint. "Why don't you and Lilly join us, too? It would do you all good to spend more time together. Lilly could help me clean up after dinner and the two of you could go someplace and talk."

"Well, that does sound good," Maegan said.

Clint nodded. "Dinner would be great."

He wished Mrs. Hargrove could invite King Solomon to dinner, too. They could sure use some of that kind of wisdom when it came to deciding Lilly's future.

"You're staying for church, aren't you?" Clint said as he turned to Maegan. "Lilly is saving a place for you."

Maegan didn't hesitate more than a moment before she nodded. She wasn't sure she was ready to hear more about God, but she didn't want to disappoint her niece.

"Is there anything I need to know?" she asked Clint quickly as Mrs. Hargrove started walking away from them, muttering something about finding Charlie. "Kneeling? Standing?"

"Don't worry. We don't stand on ceremony here. You'll do fine. Just follow everyone else."

Someone started playing the piano softly as soon as Maegan slid into the pew beside Lilly. The girl had arranged for her to sit on one side of her and Clint on the other. The sun finally began to shine outside and the rays filtered in through the side windows. A wooden cross was hanging in the front of the church and it looked like it had been polished recently.

The pastor, Matthew Curtis, started to talk and Maegan listened. He said he had been angry with God when his first wife had died of cancer. He felt like God hadn't answered his prayer and that meant God didn't care about him. After years of being miserable, he realized God still loved him. Not all answers to prayer were the ones people wanted, he finally said. Sometimes the answers people received meant they needed to trust God more than they believed they could.

Maegan had to blink back her tears a couple of times when she was listening. She had thought she was the only one who had been angry at God. And to have a church man admit that he'd felt the same way brought her comfort.

By the time the church service was over, she was glad she was going to be spending some time with others. The pastor's talk had made her feel warmer and she had shaken half a dozen hands as she stood in the entryway to the church. The pastor's new wife, Glory, had greeted her warmly, too. It was all just so perfect. Maegan wished she had those little confetti pieces to scatter over the people of Dry Creek. They were good people and should be celebrated.

The whole world looked like a more hopeful place today. Part of that was because her niece held her hand while they walked over to Mrs. Hargrove's house. The other part was that Clint was walking on the other side of her. It struck her as they were making their way up the steps to the house that this was the closest she had come to feeling like she was part of a family since her own had been taken from her. Of course, it was all very temporary, but it felt good.

Lilly was winning her heart. The girl was gripping her hand fiercely. Or maybe it was Maegan squeezing her niece's hand. Either way, it was a good day. They were together and they were going to have dinner with people who cared about them. There was nothing more Maegan could ask of a day. Unless, of course— She looked at Clint again. She wondered if someone like him and someone like her could ever— No, she decided. She'd be happy with what she had now. She'd never really been part of a family. She wouldn't know how to even go about it. It was safer just to think of Lilly.

Chapter Four

Clint shifted his weight on the chair so he could look over his shoulder and see the clock hanging above his refrigerator. It was midafternoon on Monday and he still had a good, long hour before he needed to pick up Lilly from school. The minutes were dragging. After dinner yesterday, Mrs. Hargrove had suggested he and Maegan get together and talk about each other's parenting styles so they could think about Lilly's future more objectively.

That's what they were doing now and, five minutes into it, it was a disaster.

It had sounded so civilized when Mrs. Hargrove mentioned the conversation. But here they were, both leaning their elbows on the kitchen table and avoiding even looking at each other. Clint drummed his fingers lightly on the scarred wood and wished he could remember some reassuring stories from his childhood that showed he had parenting potential. When he couldn't do that, he wished he was sitting someplace else, maybe outside in the barn with the horses. Or even with the chickens.

He realized he didn't want anyone to know much about his past, especially not a woman whose opinion of him was beginning to matter. But he could hardly plead the Fifth without looking guilty. He glanced over at Maegan and wondered if she had noticed he'd pressed the shirt he was wearing. Ironing wasn't on top of the priority list for most bachelor ranchers, at least not on a day when they didn't even leave their places.

He had been worried that the white dress shirt might seem too formal until he'd opened his door and saw that Maegan had shown up in the same maroon suit she'd worn to church. She could have been going to a bank to apply for a loan instead of sitting down with a friend to discuss things. He didn't want that to offend him, but it did a little. Then he heard the shrill whistle of his kettle.

He jumped up and went to the stove.

Maegan had said yesterday that she liked tea and this morning he'd pulled his mother's old teapot out of the back cupboard and washed it up so it was ready to use. He hoped the beverage would relax her. He'd even put a plate of graham crackers on the table. They were the closest thing he had to cookies and Lilly liked them fine. Maegan didn't even look at the plate. She had her yellow tablet in front of her and seemed determined to take notes on whatever conclusions they reached.

At the stove, he poured the hot water into the pot and dangled a few tea bags into it. He put the lid back on and balanced the pot in his hands as he brought it back to the table. Maegan started looking around the table and he finally realized she was looking for something to set under the pot. His home didn't run to such niceties as trivets and coasters.

He wasn't used to entertaining, but he suddenly wished he'd covered the oak table with a cloth or at least moved it away from the light that shone directly down on it, highlighting every imperfection. Sitting in the middle of the kitchen like it had for decades, it had collected black scars from hot skillets and wavy circles from water sitting too long on the varnish. His family had always been ranchers and the land had come first. No one had cared about keeping the table looking good and, by the time it became his inheritance, it seemed pointless to protect it after so many decades of hard use.

Clint set the teapot on the table without apology.

He was sure there was a lace tablecloth in the upstairs closet that had belonged to his grandmother. He'd never gone through that particular closet to throw anything away so it must be still there. Although maybe having a nice tablecloth would just make the rest of the house look shabbier.

"Smells good," Maegan finally said as she eyed the teapot and twisted the pen in her hand.

"Please," Clint said as he gestured to the mugs. "Help yourself."

She still looked nervous to him. Well, that made two of them. He didn't know what to say, either. If he didn't think he'd look like he had something to hide, he'd suggest they call the whole thing off.

Finally, Maegan reached for one of the clean mugs Clint kept in the middle of the table right beside the salt and pepper. He'd found it helpful to keep the mugs there, but he hadn't thought how messy it might look to someone else, especially with his unpaid bills pressed between them and a small jar of sugar to the side.

"I should have gotten out the china cups." The cups and teapot with their tiny pink rose-buds and gold rims were the only things in the house that had belonged to his mother until cancer claimed her. Maybe that's why he and his brother kept them tucked away. It seemed like their mother had come and gone in this house like a vapor. It was his father's family who had lived and died within these walls for generations. "Those cups go with the teapot."

He didn't think he'd ever been so nervous around a woman. Of course, no woman had ever judged his fitness for anything in quite the same way. He wasn't going to apologize though. He was a rancher and new thrashing equipment had come before fixing up the kitchen in the budget. Maybe with Lilly here he needed to change his priorities, but he had time to do that. "You can put that in the minus column for me. It seems I've never paid proper attention to tableware—and the kitchen in general. Lilly would probably like the rose cups. I'll see to that, but for now you can count it against me."

Maegan had already marked the four columns on the top sheet of her tablet, a plus and minus column for each of them. But she didn't make a move to add anything to either column. Instead, she poured herself a cup of the tea. "I'm sure Lilly can live with whatever dishes you normally use. We need to focus on the important things about being a parent."

Clint had been afraid she'd say something like that. He'd rather gut the house and rebuild it than air his more personal shortcomings. He wondered sometimes if that wasn't part of the reason he'd stopped joining in with folks for church and things. No one could see his faults if he kept to himself. Of course, Lilly coming changed everything. She needed to be around people and so he took her places.

"Mrs. Hargrove said we needed to start with family histories, but we can wait if you'd rather," Maegan said as she took a sip of tea.

"We might as well start there as anywhere." He inhaled deeply. He might have let the house go some, but he was an honest man. He'd say what needed to be said. "My mother is the one who had the rose teacups that go with the teapot. She died when I was young, but she must have liked nice things. Girl things."

He was going to continue, but Maegan wrote "teacups/pot" on the plus column under his name and then looked up at him. "She sounds like a lovely person."

"I'm sure she was," Clint said after a moment's hesitation. He never talked about his mother, but he had fleeting impressions that visited him now and again on a winter night as he relaxed by the fire in the living room. "I remember she used to laugh, especially on a day like this with the sun coming into the kitchen. She'd always push the curtains out of the way so the light could come in and open the doors to the outside. Then she'd pick me up and swirl me around the kitchen."

"And your dad?"

"He used to bring us presents." And it was true. His father had managed to keep himself together somehow for the first few years after his wife died, but then the crops failed one year when Clint was about eight and the combination of that and his grief broke something in him. After that, he would go on benders for a week or two, leaving his sons alone. Clint and his brother wouldn't know if the man was dead or alive until he'd show up at the door all weepy-eyed and holding out some cheap present he'd bought for them when he'd sobered up enough to think about where he was and who might be back on the farm with nothing to eat.

"That sounds so nice," Maegan said and the longing in her voice brought him up short.

"The presents were never much," Clint admitted. He didn't really want to mislead anyone even if he could never squeeze the whole truth out. "Some of those mugs are from him. I don't think we have any of the other things he gave us but they were mostly candy or maybe a plastic toy for Joe. Once he bought us caramel apples."

Clint didn't add that fortunately the school bus came to the ranch back in those days and Joe was old enough to go to an all-day kindergarten some of the parents had put together. They managed to get themselves to school, more for the free lunch than anything else. Their hair and clothes might not have been clean, but they hadn't aroused any suspicions.

"I got my barrette from my mother," Maegan said with a smile as she reached up to touch the knot of hair on her head. "It wasn't much, either, but I still have it."

Clint watched as her hands fluttered around her head.

"Your hair is beautiful." The words came out of his mouth before he realized what he was saying. She looked at him in surprise and he swallowed. "I mean, with the barrette and all. It looks real nice."

"Thank you," she said and smiled. "I

remember my mother brushing my hair at night. I can't remember her face, but I'll never forget the feel of the brush on my head and the sense of peace I felt just being with her."

They were quiet for a moment, each lost in their own memories.

"Lilly doesn't like the way I fix her hair," Clint finally admitted. "You better put that in the minus column for me and the plus column for you."

"I don't think I should get a plus just because you get a minus," Maegan said as she made a check on her tablet. "I've never combed Lilly's hair."

Clint smiled. "She likes it braided. Not the way I braid it, of course, but the way her mother used to do it. The way anyone with any fashion sense would do it, according to her."

Maegan chuckled and reached for her mug. "She's at that age where she's a little self-conscious about her looks. And with her feet. I had the same problem."

"Well, you turned out all right. That makes me feel better."

They were silent as she took another sip of tea then carefully set the mug back down on the table.

"I'm afraid I—" Maegan's voice broke and

she stopped only to start again, her voice so soft Clint had to lean forward to hear her. "I'm afraid I wouldn't be a very good parent no matter how much she and I have in common."

She looked down at her cup after she had spoken. The lines in her face were strained. Her eyes were suspiciously damp. "It doesn't matter what's on my list. I'm just not—"

"No," Clint said as he reached for her. He didn't want her to continue. "You're being too hard on yourself." He swallowed. "And, I haven't been—well, I didn't learn how to be a good parent, either. My father was a drunk. The only reason no one took us away from him was because we were too scared of him to even tell our teachers. I forged his signature when I had to and told everyone he was sick on the nights of the school plays. I did the best I could to keep Joe going to school and fed, but he was—well, he left school anyway before he could graduate from high school. He blames me for a lot of what he's missed in life—and he might be right."

"You?" Maegan asked, her voice rising at the end of the word in what could be either surprise or indignation. "Why would he blame you? How old were you anyway?"

"I would have been eight when my father started leaving us alone."

"Goodness, you were just a kid."

"Maybe," Clint agreed. "But I was almost four years older than him. I should have done something to get us help."

"You would have only been put in the foster care system," Maegan said. "That might not have been much better than what you had right here."

"But I didn't even try," Clint said and paused. He'd never even admitted this to himself, but the truth was staring him in the face. "I kept thinking my dad would change. I remember him when my mom was alive. I kept thinking if we just held out a little longer, we would have our dad back, the way he used to be. Everything would be okay then."

They were both silent for a moment.

"So, yeah, it was my fault we didn't get any help," Clint muttered finally and then added in a firmer voice. "You better put that on your list. It's a big one, too. Poor judgment when it comes to other people. A sucker for a lost cause."

Clint started to push himself up from the table. That pretty well summed up his fears in life. He didn't even have to mention the disaster of his engagement. He just wasn't someone who had the usual kind of relationships. He thought Maegan might understand that. But then he saw her pick up her pen and he sat down again. She wrote "loved father" in bold, black letters on his plus column.

"I loved my parents, too," she whispered when she set the pen down. She looked Clint straight in the eyes. "They died and left me, but I still felt the same way about them. I was angry at them for a while, but nobody could replace them for me. It wouldn't have mattered if they'd become drunks. They would have still been my parents. I'd have hoped they would change just like you did with your father."

Maegan looked down when she finished. Her eyes had blazed with emotion when she'd spoke and Clint suspected that some of the glow in her eyes was from tears that were forming. Sure enough, one started to slide down her cheek.

The clouds outside must have turned gray because the light streaming through the kitchen windows had lost its shine. The dampness in the air promised rain. Only the overhead light shone down on them.

Everything in the kitchen had turned delicate. The clock ticked in the background. The tea was growing cold in the mug. Maegan looked fragile, her skin pale and her eyes downcast as though she was fighting the sorrow that caused her tear to flow. Clint felt like he should turn around and give her some privacy. He couldn't help himself though. He moved his chair closer and reached over to wipe away the tear.

Maegan sat there, trying to take a deep breath. "I think I might have hay fever."

His thumb rested on her cheek and he tilted her face up with the rest of his hand. "It's not the season for hay. But it's all right."

She looked at him again, her eyes shimmering and her face flushed. Her skin was so soft he caressed her cheek lightly with his thumb.

"Maybe I have a speck in my eye then. Truly, I never cry."

"There's nothing wrong with a few tears." Clint struggled to find words for all of the other things he suddenly wanted to say, but all he could come up with was, "You're entitled to them."

Maegan closed her eyes then and he hoped it was from relief.

"You and me, we know how hard life can be," he said and then added because he thought it might make her feel better, "That part about me hoping my father would turn back into his old self, I've never told that to anyone. Not even Joe. I always felt a little foolish for believing it was even possible. I hate to feel like a fool."

Maegan nodded and another tear slid down her cheek. He let it collect on the side of his thumb before rubbing the dampness against her cheek. She was soft as a peach.

"It was hard being the oldest," Maegan whispered into his hand. "I felt I should save my sisters somehow and I couldn't even save myself. Our family was destroyed and I couldn't do anything to stop it."

"I know," Clint said. "Believe me, I know."

Then he did the only thing he could. He slid his chair close enough that he could put his arm around her. She leaned into him willingly and something eased in his heart as he held her tight. He felt someone understood him at long last.

They sat there, shoulder to shoulder, for a long time. A crack of thunder sounded outside and a slow rain beat against the roof. Then for no good reason Clint bent over and kissed her on the top of her head. He cared about her and the surprise of it shot through him. He hadn't thought he could feel so protective of someone.

* * *

She felt his lips press against her hair again. What had ever made her think a column of pluses and minuses would show who was worthy to raise a child? Her mother used to kiss her like that when she came in to say good-night. Maegan looked up to meet Clint's eyes, planning to tell him that and to thank him for reminding her of her mother's kiss. But everything shifted when she saw his eyes. They were dark, even with the light shining down on them from overhead. And they swirled with emotion. There was nothing of her mother in this man's eyes.

She knew he was going to kiss her—really kiss her—even before he leaned closer to her. She expected to feel a moment's panic. She didn't make a habit of kissing men she hadn't known for long. But his lips, the moment they met hers, felt right. And then she felt him pull away.

The room seemed to grow colder as he moved his chair back to his original place at the table.

Then he looked over at her aghast. "I'm sorry. I know that was unexpected. I wouldn't want you to think I'm trying to sway your opinion of me, as far as Lilly is concerned or anything."

"Oh," Maegan said. She hadn't been able to form a coherent thought after the kiss and she was a little miffed that he could. Then she saw the bewildered look on his face. He hadn't figured on a kiss like that any more than she had.

Somehow the sure knowledge that he didn't go around kissing people any more than she did made her calm. She picked up her mug again. "It wouldn't matter if you were trying to influence me. I already think you're doing the best you can for my niece."

They were both silent for a moment, just looking at each other.

Then Clint moved and started to get up from his chair. "Your tea is probably cold. I better heat up some more water for you."

Maegan nodded and cleared her throat. "More tea would be nice."

She didn't say that tea always settled her nerves. She had a feeling something major had happened with that kiss, but she didn't have the words to talk about it. There was no need to mention it anyway; he didn't seem to have anything more to say. And she could hardly say her world had shifted. She certainly would never look at Clint again and think he was too busy to care about Lilly. He might not believe he had what was needed to raise Lilly, but Maegan was becoming convinced he did. His heart was filled with emotions that didn't show on his face.

She watched him move around the kitchen as he filled the kettle with more water for the tea. She hadn't noticed until now the crayon pictures on the refrigerator. Three bright stick figures that stood in front of a small house.

"Lilly's work?" she asked and pointed.

Clint turned from the stove to see what she meant. "Yeah, they're pictures of her mom and her."

Maegan looked more closely. "The third figure must be her brother."

"Her brother?" Clint turned to her in surprise. "I thought the other stick figure was a dog or something. It's so much smaller than the other two. I didn't know she has a brother."

Maegan nodded. "A half brother. Wesley is about four, living with his father down in Texas. I don't know if she saw much of him. The history was a little muddled, but it sounded like his father might have started raising him when he was a baby. I can't believe Dawn would give up her own son completely though—she must have had some kind of visitation with him. If she did, Lilly would be there."

Maegan stopped and thought. "I just assumed you'd know. Hasn't she mentioned him?"

Clint shook his head and walked back over to the table. "Not to me. I don't know—maybe she said something to Joe, but he didn't pass the word along. That could be true—he didn't mention you, either, and here you are."

They were both silent for a moment.

"The poor thing," Maegan finally said. "All those years when she was in foster care, she had a brother. I wonder if she thought Wesley had died, too."

"Oh, I hope not. She's already lost so much," Clint muttered as he shook his head. "I probably should have asked if she had any other family. I just never thought— What kind of a man doesn't even ask?"

"You're doing the best you can," Maegan said. "I'm not sure I would have asked, either. I would have just assumed someone would have said something if she had a sibling."

They sat and let the kettle heat. Neither one of them wanted any tea. Maegan realized she was counting on Clint to be the parent. She felt helpless. She wished there was a university she could attend to learn about how to be a good parent. She'd always been good with books; maybe she could learn what she needed to know. She'd do that if Lilly needed her.

"Maybe she mentioned her brother to Mrs. Hargrove," Clint finally said. "I've never seen kids take to anyone like they do to her. They spill all their secrets when they're around her. It's part of what makes her such a good Sunday school teacher. Maybe we should ask her about this."

"She'll know what we should do," Maegan said in relief. She wished she had thought of the older woman. "I wonder if she's home now."

"Likely." Clint looked at the clock and then stood up. He walked over to the stove and turned the burner off under the kettle. "I should be heading into Dry Creek anyway in a bit. The school bus brings the kids from the school in Miles City and drops them off at the café. Then the parents pick them up from there. The district can't afford to have the bus take them to the ranches anymore. Gas is too expensive."

"I'll follow you in," Maegan said as she gathered up her tablet and stood up as well.

They stood facing each other for a moment, but neither one of them made eye contact.

"We need to see to Lilly first," Clint said, his voice low and troubled.

Maegan nodded as she reached for the purse she'd draped over one of the chairs. She didn't ask him what he meant by saying they needed to do something first. What was second? Them? Surely not, but she wasn't sure she was prepared to hear his answer if she asked the question. Telling each other secrets from their childhoods had made them feel temporarily close. She knew that, but she didn't want to talk about it.

She'd never had feelings like this and they were fragile. She could count on her fingers the number of people who had understood her in her life. People from real homes never got it. They didn't know how she felt. But Clint did. And it made her feel good. She wanted to hug the moment tight for just a little longer before ordinary life returned.

Chapter Five

Clint and Maegan were sitting in Mrs. Hargrove's kitchen. He had called her before they headed into Dry Creek so, when they arrived, the older woman already had hot water for tea. She poured some for Maegan and asked if he wanted coffee. There was a big plate of shortbread cookies in the middle of the table and a wicker basket with assorted tea bags. A glass with a pitcher of cold milk sat ready to pour when Lilly walked in the front door. He had already stopped at the café to ask Linda to tell his niece to come over here when she got off the school bus.

The coziness of the setting did not deceive Clint. His nerves were on edge. He didn't say anything about the problem though.

"Nice cloth," he said instead as he fingered the slick green-and-white-checked cloth that hung over the edges of the table. He could learn something here. There was nothing elegant about Mrs. Hargrove's kitchen, but it sure was a whole sight more welcoming than the one at his ranch. Part of it might be the way the air smelled. The older woman had made bread earlier that day and the tea Maegan had chosen was orange spice. The combination made a person feel at home.

"I've got to say the oilcloth sure works for spills," Mrs. Hargrove agreed as she stood by the stove pouring a cup of coffee. "I always think a kitchen table should expect its share of tipsy things so I save the delicate coverings for the dining room. No one should have to worry about ruining anything when they're eating in the kitchen. They can even put their elbows on the table and talk sports for all I care."

Clint nodded. He knew Mrs. Hargrove had come to accept sports a little more now that she was married again and Charlie was a fan. Clint didn't expect Lilly to want to talk about football, but maybe someday she'd open up about what excited her. "I'm going to get one of those tablecloths. You call them oilcloths? Maybe I can find one with some flowers on it. Lilly likes yellow. At least, that's the color she always picks when we buy those new thing-a-majiggies—ties, she calls them—for her hair."

All of a sudden, the thought of Lilly and her hair depressed him. He should be able to braid a little bit of hair. No tablecloth could make up for his fumbling fingers. If it was horse hair, he knew he could do a good job, but a little girl squirmed in the chair and her hair was so soft it flew every which way.

Just thinking about it, he looked at Maegan. She'd twisted her hair back into the same kind of knot she'd worn earlier—well, earlier as in before they kissed. He remembered it looked significantly messier when they left his kitchen twenty minutes ago. If she could bring that amount of order back with the little mirror in her car, she could do anything Lilly wanted.

Maegan chose that moment to look up and meet his eyes. He almost blinked at the raw vulnerability he saw in her. He knew without her saying anything that the tea she was drinking hadn't soothed her feelings. Lilly and her brother were getting to her. Losing her sisters had pained Maegan almost as much as losing her parents, partly because he knew she felt she should be able to do something to keep them together. Now she was worried Lilly carried the same burden for her brother.

"It's not the same—" he whispered before her chin came up and a curtain fell over her eyes. She didn't want him to say anything.

He kept his mouth silent, but he couldn't stop his heart. *God, don't let her do this to herself,* he prayed. *We don't even know that it's the same for Lilly.*

Maegan was quiet. She looked like a fierce statue, protecting herself. And, with the strength of it all, she was so beautiful that the breath seeped out of his lungs and his brain shut down. He forgot what he was thinking or praying about. Then she moved slightly and it all came flooding back. Oh, yes, her hair. She had the most rich-looking hair he'd ever seen. Golden honey-blond and he knew it felt like silk to a man's hand because he'd touched it when they kissed.

He stopped himself. This wasn't smart. He was a bachelor rancher, not some young girl who fell in love with everyone who waltzed by. He must need to date more if the glance of a beautiful woman did this to him. Not that it was just any glance he knew. Still, he needed to rein things in.

His ears slowly cleared and he heard Mrs. Hargrove talking as she pushed her coffee-maker back to the wall.

"Of course, the grocery store in Miles City

also has them if you can't get to Billings," the older woman continued just like the air hadn't been sucked out of the room and pumped back in with stardust in it. Then she walked back to the table, holding a cup of coffee for Clint and a cup of hot water for herself. "You'll see the sign right next to the spices. It says 'imported oilcloth.'"

"I know where that is," Clint said, hoping his relief wasn't evident. He needed to focus. He remembered he'd been so busy in the barn that he hadn't eaten lunch before Maegan had come to the ranch. Maybe the reason for all the sensations he was having was because he had some low blood sugar problem going today. "A new tablecloth—Lilly would like one of them." He wondered if he had already said that. He didn't want to sound like an idiot so he added, "Kids need some color around them."

Maegan nodded at that. She looked like she had found her footing again, too. Like their eyes had never met and melded. Her voice was precise and professional. "Well, you already have Lilly's drawings so you know she likes color."

Clint felt his whole face tighten. Maybe he should say something about all that was happening between him and Maegan, but he couldn't. Not in front of Mrs. Hargrove.

"Oh, I didn't know Lilly was a little artist," the older woman said and then put a tea bag in her cup. "Outside of doing the beading on her bridle, I've never seen her do anything."

"She hasn't shown you her drawings?" Maegan asked. There was some urgency in her voice and all thoughts of the kiss were gone in Clint's mind as she continued. "The family of stick figures?"

"No, I'm sure I would remember if she had." Mrs. Hargrove looked at Maegan and then Clint. "Am I missing something?"

"It's my fault," Clint said, not bothering to list the many ways in which it was. He hadn't looked close enough at the drawings to see that what he thought was a dog might be a boy. He had made Maegan anxious or, at least, hadn't done anything to stop her fears. "I should have known Lilly had a brother."

"Ohhh," Mrs. Hargrove said and her mouth formed the perfect letter to match. It seemed to take her a minute, but she rallied. "I had no idea. She never said. A brother, you say?"

Clint nodded. "We're not sure Lilly knows much about him, but we think she must because she drew this."

He reached in his pocket and pulled out the

drawing that had hung on his refrigerator earlier. He unfolded it and laid it on the table.

Mrs. Hargrove reached over and picked it up. She studied it a minute and then nodded. "The hair on the small stick figure does look like a boy's. He's the one?"

Maegan nodded. "We think so. My sister Olivia and I found out about the two children when we discovered our youngest sister, Dawn, had died in a car accident. The foster care system record was pretty sketchy, but Wesley, that's who we think is the boy in the picture." She pointed to Lilly's drawing. "He's the youngest of the two and has been living with his father in Texas—I think since he was born."

She paused for a moment and then continued. "After I thought about it some, I'm not really surprised Dawn gave up custody. She was in foster care for a few years before she was adopted and that might not have gone all that well. I'm sure she thought she'd be a terrible mother. I've thought that about myself. But I can't believe Dawn didn't visit the boy sometimes. And she probably took Lilly with her when she went. Besides, a child like Lilly would want to have a brother. She might romanticize him even if she didn't know him."

"Like she'd done with Joe," Clint added, his lips twisting.

"Exactly like that," Mrs. Hargrove said, her face thoughtful. "But she knows where her father is. I wonder though what she thinks happened to her brother."

"She sure hasn't said anything to me about him, or to Maegan," Clint said, not bothering to hide his discouragement. "Or apparently to you."

They were all silent for a moment then Maegan looked at the others and asked, "That's not normal, is it? I mean, assuming she knows. Why wouldn't she tell anyone she has a brother? Or ask questions about him? Is she mad at us or something?"

"Oh, I don't think she's angry," Mrs. Hargrove said quickly. "She might be a quiet child, but she isn't acting out. She hasn't tried running away—"

"Running away? I never thought she might try to leave." Clint felt cold shivers run down his back. He felt a strong urge to build a tall fence around his land with a locked gate. "She's only nine years old."

"Yes, well, she probably wouldn't get far," the older woman conceded.

"Unless someone took advantage of her and—" Maegan's voice started to rise. But then she stopped and swallowed, keeping her eyes downcast.

Clint reached out and put his hand on her arm. "She's okay. She's with us."

He'd put in that fence if he needed to.

Maegan looked up at him in surprise. "Us?"

He nodded firmly. He wanted this much understood; he wasn't in some fog when it came to the two of them. "You're Lilly's aunt. You're part of her future now, too."

He didn't add that he hoped she was also part of his future. He didn't want to give her any excuses to pick up and leave.

Maegan knew there were certain moments in a person's life when everything changed. This was such a moment. It was right up there with the time all those years ago when she realized the couple she'd prayed would be perfect for her family disappointed her. They were not going to do anything to keep her sisters and her together after all. God had seemed so far away back then when she yearned to keep her family close.

But now everything was shifting. God seemed to be answering those old prayers. She might not have both of her sisters, but Olivia and she were becoming closer every day as they talked on the phone. And she had a connection with Lilly. If Clint said she could be part of the girl's life, she knew he meant it. A flood of warm emotions went through her with that knowledge. She finally had family— sort of.

"Thank you." Maegan let enough silence pass to let everyone know she recognized the gift Clint was offering.

Mrs. Hargrove nodded, her weathered face beaming as she looked at her and then at Clint. "Now, isn't this nice? The two of you joining forces to see to your niece. It's almost like—"

"We'll have to ask her about her brother," Maegan added quickly, before the older woman could say more. She wasn't ready for any kind of scrutiny when it came to her feelings about Clint. Being permitted to see more of her niece was enough for now. "Maybe Lilly just doesn't talk about Wesley because she's worried."

"That could be," Clint admitted.

"Or maybe she saw him so seldom, she wasn't expecting to see him again," Maegan said before she heard what sounded like a truck drive by.

"That'll be the school bus," Mrs. Hargrove said as she stood and walked over to the kitchen window that faced the street. "It needs to have the engine adjusted—my nephew Conrad is supposed to fix the problem, but he's away for a week learning how to repair some new-fangled fuel-efficient tractor. He took his new wife and they're making it a little vacation. You know how it is—young love? He never thought he'd get married, either."

With the last, the older woman turned around and beamed some more as she looked toward the table. Fortunately, she kept her thoughts to herself though.

Maegan stood up and walked over to the window so she could look out. The yellow bus had a black stripe. Square windows lined its sides and there was a bear painted on the driver's door.

Mrs. Hargrove must have known where Maegan was looking. "The basketball players are the Grizzlies. They use the bus to get the kids to the games. They even play a school up at Havre."

Maegan watched as the children stepped off the school bus. They were boisterous, jumping around and running to the café. Lilly lagged behind the others, walking slow as though she carried the weight of the world on her shoulders. Even with her limp, she could go faster than she was.

"She's not happy." Clint had come to stand by the window, too, and he saw what the women did. "I've tried everything I know and she's just not happy."

"Give her time," Mrs. Hargrove replied. She was no longer smiling and her voice was worried even though her words were sympathetic. "She hasn't dealt with losing her mother and she was just brought hundreds of miles across the country to live with someone she had never met before. She needs time to adjust."

For a minute, they just listened to the sound of the children outside.

"I'm going to paint the house at the ranch," Clint said suddenly. "Inside and out. Bright colors, too. Maybe that will help some. Right after the days dry out enough so there's no chance of rain."

"But what about the spring plowing?" Mrs. Hargrove turned and asked. "As soon as it's dry enough, that's what you'll need to be doing."

"I'll paint at night," Clint said, his voice strong with determination. "Or put it off for a day or two."

Maegan was only partially listening. She saw Lilly enter the café, following a group of other kids.

"I know how the girl feels." She stepped

away from the window. She knew some of the reason Lilly trailed behind was because of her feet. It was hard to keep up when she had to be so careful with the way she walked. Added to that, she probably still wondered if her life was going to change again. If she was picked up and dropped off in Montana one day what was to prevent someone from picking her up tomorrow and depositing her in Nevada or Minnesota or anywhere else they desired.

"We need to sit at the table," Mrs. Hargrove said as she, too, stepped back. "We don't want her to see us watching over her like old mother hens."

Maegan smiled. She liked the thought of mothering Lilly. All of them sat down at the table again and listened quietly.

"That'll be Lilly now," Mrs. Hargrove said and stood. They had all heard the light footsteps on the front porch.

The older woman hurried out of the kitchen, walking through the dining room to get to the door coming into the living room from the porch. Maegan and Clint couldn't see her but they could hear the murmur of voices as Lilly came inside the house.

Maegan forced herself to smile as she heard Lilly nearing the entrance to the kitchen.

The girl stopped in the doorway and looked at Clint and Maegan. "Am I in trouble?"

"Oh, no," Maegan gasped. But then she noticed that Lilly had her eye on Clint and she was waiting for his response. The girl was uncertain.

"Not at all," Clint said softly and he opened his arms to Lilly.

The girl didn't go to him, but the worried look left her face and she said, "Oh. Well, then, Mrs. Hargrove said I could have some cookies."

"That I did," the older woman said as she, too, entered the kitchen.

With that, Lilly started taking off her gray parka as she walked to the table. She draped the coat over the back of her chair before starting to sit down.

"That's my picture," she said stiffly, pausing midway to the chair. She straightened herself and kept standing as she looked at Clint again.

Maegan could see the hurt and confusion in Clint's eyes. Lilly was acting like she expected him to harshly reprimand her for something. Maegan knew Clint well enough now to assume that he was never unkind to anyone, and especially not to Lilly.

"I tried not to use much crayon," Lilly said defensively. "I know they're not cheap."

"You can have all the crayons you want," Clint said, his voice cracking with defeat. "And paper, too—whatever you need."

Lilly nodded. She sat down and folded her hands.

There was an awkward silence.

"Well, land's sake, child, have a cookie," Mrs. Hargrove finally said as she pulled her own chair out and sat down. "You must be starving. I know they give you lunch at school, but it's never enough."

"We had hot dogs today," Lilly said, relaxing as she talked to the older woman. "And carrot sticks."

"Sounds good," Mrs. Hargrove said as she poured the glass of milk and pushed the plate of cookies closer to Lilly. "Go ahead now. I know these are your favorite."

Lilly nodded shyly as she reached her hand out.

Maegan and Clint didn't say anything as their niece took bites around the edge of the sugar cookie, methodically making it smaller and smaller until there was only one round bite left. She sat that on her napkin and took a long drink of the milk.

"I expect all kids like to have a snack when

they get home from school." Mrs. Hargrove smiled at Lilly. "I'm sure your Uncle Clint gives you a snack, too."

Lilly nodded. "Mostly graham crackers, sitting at the kitchen table. He gets them just for me, because I like them."

Maegan relaxed and addressed herself to Lilly. "I was out at your place this afternoon. I think I even had some of your graham crackers. They were very nice."

Lilly smiled.

Maegan looked over at Clint and he gave her a subtle nod so she continued. "That's when I saw the picture you drew. It's a very nice picture and I was wondering if you could tell me about it."

Maegan reached out and moved the drawing closer to the girl.

Lilly was sober. "Did you know my mother?"

Maegan shook her head slightly. "Not really. She was very young when we got sent to different places to live. I wish I had known her later though. She must have been a good mother to have a daughter like you."

Lilly stiffened and looked down at the table. "She said she was a bad mother. That's why she was looking for my father. She wanted to send me to live with him."

"Oh, surely—" Maegan was taken back. She hadn't expected any of this. What kind of a woman had her sister been? "Maybe she meant she wanted you to spend some time with your father. Like visiting for a few weeks in the summer."

Lilly just sat there for a moment, then she took a deep breath and continued. "She told me she'd already given my brother to his father. He was just a baby, but I saw him. I used to think about my brother all the time. I bet he's happy, being with his dad."

Everything stopped and no one breathed for a long minute.

Then Lilly dropped her voice and said listlessly, "I'll be happy, too, when I can live with my father."

Maegan felt all of the hope drain out of her. How could Lilly want to be with the man who had left her with his brother? Clint had hinted that his brother wasn't ready to take care of a child and it was clear the man might never be ready. And then there was her. She knew she shouldn't have started to count on having a relationship with Lilly, but she did. Just the thought of it had made her realize how much she wanted to be part of a family again. Even if she only visited Lilly and Clint now and then, it would be something. But how would she even find Lilly if she was going from rodeo to rodeo?

Just then Mrs. Hargrove moved slightly.

"Your uncle's very nice, too," the older woman said gently as she put her hand on Lilly's shoulder and drew the girl closer to her.

Lilly didn't say anything. She just looked down.

Maegan looked over at Clint. His face was drained. He looked as bereft as she felt. She reached out and put her hand on his arm. For a moment, he didn't do anything. Then he slowly put one of his hands over hers. He kept his eyes on Lilly though.

"I wish I was your dad," he said to the girl, his voice ragged.

Lilly still didn't say anything. And that, Maegan thought to herself, said it all. The girl wasn't happy. Nothing but her father would do. It was unfortunate, but she could understand. Hadn't she felt the same way one time? She wanted what she wanted in a family and, if she couldn't have it, she didn't want much of anything else.

She could almost see the same thoughts chasing through Clint's mind. Then she saw his face harden with resolve.

"I'll talk to your father," Clint finally said.

Lilly looked up then, her face filled with hope. "You will?"

Clint swallowed. "I promise. I'll do everything I can to get the two of you together."

It was then that Lilly went to Clint and hugged him around his waist. He bent down and kissed her on the head. Maegan held her own emotions in check. She knew that if Lilly went back with her dad, the likelihood was that she wouldn't see much of her niece. Or—she looked over to the two of them—of Clint, either. The fragile family she seemed to be collecting was starting to scatter before it could even form. She wasn't ready to lose what she'd barely found.

Chapter Six

Even though Maegan felt tired right down to her bones, she couldn't sleep. She'd gone to bed early, hoping to fall into a deep slumber and wake up in the morning ready to do what she needed to do. She was going to stop Lilly from living with her father again. The girl couldn't possibly want to live with that man. Clint had told her that his brother had left Lilly at the ranch without much of a backward glance. Did the girl really want to live with him? What kind of a life would she have if she did? Would Maegan ever see her niece again if that happened? Would Joe even take care of his daughter if she was traveling around with him? Would he even let her come with him?

The list of worries was endless. Maegan suspected she could get a judge to agree it was in Lilly's best interests to be raised by her or

Clint. Either one of them was more stable than a wandering rodeo rider. Legal battles were fought over custody every day and Maegan could see lots of ways to twist this one in the direction she thought it should go. She had come so close to what she'd wanted all her life and it was hard to see her chance to be part of a family slip away. Shouldn't she at least fight for what she wanted? That's what the law was for.

But as convinced as her mind was on the course of action she needed to take, her heart was ambivalent. Lilly's feelings were so clear. And lying here awake only made everything worse. Remembering that Mrs. Hargrove had a small basket of tea bags, Maegan wondered if any of them were the kind that encouraged sleep. She looked at her watch. It was still early, not even nine o'clock yet, so she got up and walked over to the door. When she opened it, she saw the lights were on in the house's kitchen. She could even see that someone, probably Mrs. Hargrove, was sitting at the table.

Fortunately, Maegan was wearing an old sweat suit instead of pajamas so all she had to do was put on a jacket and her shoes before she stepped outside and walked down the stairs. The cold air hit her and, even with her heavy clothes, she instinctively folded her arms across her chest to gain more warmth. With every step she took, the ground cracked slightly so she knew ice was forming in places where water had spread over the ground earlier today. Someone must have used a hose for something. She stopped, staring for a moment at the full moon, and saw the white vapor of her breath trail away as she admired the night sky. Life seemed as fragile as that disappearing vapor right now.

Tea could wait for a moment, she decided. She took a few steps to her right and looked down the street. The whole town of Dry Creek was at rest and it looked like a postcard to her. The place was more charming at night than in the daytime. A single streetlight gave the handful of buildings a soft look and long shadows promised something better than what was really there. The sight gave her comfort. This town was a good place and it survived hardships. Maybe she could as well.

A gust of wind blew by and reminded her she needed to get back inside. She turned around and hurried toward the house. A porch light showed the driveway that led to the back door. She jogged the last few yards to the door and knocked with quick little taps.

Mrs. Hargrove's face appeared in the door's window and she quickly turned the knob.

"Goodness, step inside before you freeze to death," the older woman said as she opened the door fully to her kitchen. Warm light spilled out into the darkness and the faint smell of tea drew Maegan inside.

Mrs. Hargrove closed the door after her. "I hope you're warm enough in your room. Charlie adjusted the heater up there last month, but if you need more blankets, I can get some from upstairs. We have plenty so don't hesitate to let me know."

Maegan shook her head and blinked as her eyes adjusted to the brightness of the kitchen. "I'm just having some trouble sleeping and wondered if you had any of that tea that's supposed to send you off to some dreamless state. What's it called? Sleepy something."

"Sleep Tonight tea." The older woman smiled. "Charlie uses it. I'm not surprised you're having a hard time nodding off. We've had quite the day, haven't we?"

Maegan nodded and tried to think of something else to say. She couldn't.

"Don't worry. I'm sure I have a bag of it," Mrs. Hargrove said as she turned to her table. "I've got some hot water on the stove, too.

I always have a cup of tea—or sometimes cocoa—as I sit here and read my Bible."

For the first time, Maegan looked at the table and saw the large black Bible lying open on top of the oilcloth Clint had been so taken with earlier today. "Oh, I'm sorry. I didn't mean to interrupt you when you're—" She gave a wave of her hand that she hoped included whatever spiritual thing the older woman had been doing.

"Oh, you're not an interruption." Mrs. Hargrove flipped through the tea bags in her basket trying to find the one she wanted. "In fact, I was just praying for you."

"Me?" Maegan squeaked. No one had ever prayed for her and, frankly, it made her nervous. Did that mean she had to do something to be sure the prayer was answered? She sure didn't want to be responsible for someone losing their faith, especially not a sweet old lady like Mrs. Hargrove. But she didn't have confidence any prayer for her would be answered.

"Oh, here it is." The older woman grinned as she held up a bag with a midnight-blue tag on it. Then she turned to the stove. "Take a seat and I'll get you a cup of water in no time at all."

Maegan carefully sat down at the table as

far from the Bible as she could get. She looked up at the older woman to say something, but Mrs. Hargrove had her back turned and was looking for a cup on the shelf over the stove.

Everything seemed normal, Maegan thought, so she relaxed and forgot the mild protest she had been going to make. But still it was only natural to want to know what Mrs. Hargrove was reading so she squinted and tried to see what part of the Bible the older woman was looking at. The text was upside down and too small for her to make it out. Which she took as a sign from God to mind her own business.

"I'm reading the Psalms," the older woman said without turning around or giving away by so much as a twitch that she knew Maegan had tried to see that for herself. "There's a lot about relying on God in the Psalms."

"Hmm," Maegan said, hoping that was a sufficient answer. She stared out the window, figuring that would show she wasn't really interested in the Psalms. In reality she wasn't too sure what they were.

"I was thinking," Mrs. Hargrove said as she turned and walked back to the table. She set down a cup filled with hot water and laid the bag with the midnight tag beside it. She paused until Maegan grew curious enough to turn and look at her. Then the older woman continued, "King David and you have a lot in common."

"Huh?"

Maegan's open skepticism didn't stop the older woman. She kept on talking. "He was a king back then. In fact, he was King Solomon's father."

"Okay." Now Maegan got the connection. She knew all about King Solomon. "You don't have to worry. I don't intend to abduct anyone. I want Lilly to be happy."

Maegan saw no reason to mention that she was prepared to take Lilly's father to court and do everything she could legally to make her niece well-adjusted in the long run instead of the short.

Mrs. Hargrove chuckled. "You've put everyone's happiness first all your life. I know you're not going to deliberately make Lilly unhappy." The older woman's eyes grew serious. "No, the reason you're like King David is because you're disappointed with God."

"I wouldn't exactly say I am disappointed," Maegan finally had to admit. "I'm just more your usual 'it doesn't work for me' kind of person. No harm, no foul. I mean, I believe to a point. I know God does things—"

"Just not for you," Mrs. Hargrove said in a

matter-of-fact voice as she sat back down in her chair by the Bible.

"I don't blame God for that."

"Well, you should. If that was what He was doing. But He's never ignored you."

Maegan snorted. Really, what did a person say when they couldn't say anything without seeming impolite to a woman old enough to be their grandmother? But Mrs. Hargrove had it wrong. God had never done anything for Maegan Shay. If she wanted something done, she had to do it herself.

Mrs. Hargrove seemed unruffled. "It's not even God that you're mad at. It's you. Until you forgive yourself, you won't be able to see God for who He is."

"I don't think—" Maegan began and then stopped. A single clear thought struck a note deep inside her. Something sounded so right and everything cascaded into place. Could it be true?

"It wasn't your fault you couldn't keep your family together." Mrs. Hargrove gently touched her hand. "You were only a child yourself. That didn't mean He loved you and your sisters any less than anyone else. He always wanted to be your Father and for you to be part of His family."

The dam broke inside of Maegan. She tried

to stop it, but she couldn't. It was true. She had been angry at God to hide the fact that she blamed herself. She knew it was bad manners to sit at someone's kitchen table and weep, but Mrs. Hargrove didn't seem to mind. She just kept patting Maegan on the hand and murmuring sympathetic sounds.

"I'm sorry, I don't—" Maegan finally managed to say. "I guess I've just had a hard day."

Mrs. Hargrove didn't say anything; she just looked at Maegan with understanding in her eyes.

"I guess maybe I did want God to care about me," Maegan finally said. "I didn't know how to make Him even look at me though."

"He saw you every second of the day," the older woman said. "Remember, His eye is on the sparrow? He's wanted to be your Father all along."

Maegan nodded. She couldn't say anything for the tears that were falling. She would love to have God for her Father. Mrs. Hargrove seemed to know that because she bent her head to pray. Then she showed her some verses in the Bible. And sat with her as she prayed for the first time in years.

An hour had passed before they started to drink their tea. By that time, Maegan knew she needed to handle the situation with her niece the way God would want her to. There would be no custody battle. At least not if Lilly and her father were meant to be together. By the time she decided this, she was back in bed and sleep came easily to her that night.

Clint was sitting at his kitchen table having a second cup of coffee when the phone rang. He'd already done the chores this morning and taken Lilly to meet the school bus. He didn't usually sit down for another cup of coffee, but he was running slowly today. He felt like a truck had run over him yesterday and he was still picking up the pieces of his heart.

It helped considerably that the person on the phone was Maegan. She told him she was willing to do whatever she could to help Lilly win a place in her father's heart, if that's what she wanted and her father was agreeable.

"I spent the night praying and came to the same conclusion," he said, surprised. Then he added, "I had rather counted on you talking me out of it though."

"Believe me, I would have if I'd talked to you last night before I had a cup of tea with Mrs. Hargrove."

"Oh, yes. That woman has a way of changing a person's opinion on things."

"She sure does."

"Between you and me, I don't like it though. I'll worry about Lilly if she's not here at the ranch. And I'll watch my brother like a hawk. If he's not nice to Lilly, I'll go wherever I have to and bring her back."

"If he's not good to her, I'll track him down, too," Maegan pledged.

Maybe because he was so tired he was cross-eyed, Clint added, "We could track them down together."

Silence greeted his words and he felt like cold water had been thrown in his face. "Not that we'd have to do it together, of course. I just meant we would be of one mind. The important thing would be that one of us would go and bring Lilly home."

Clint heard what sounded like a hiccup or a sob. "You're not crying, are you? We could handle getting Lilly back any way you want. I swear, we'll do it all your way."

There was more silence and then he heard Maegan say, "I thought maybe I could come out and help you paint your house. Remember, you wanted to paint it for Lilly."

"I don't think painting the house is going to make any difference to her."

"I have to do something."

Clint nodded, even though Maegan couldn't see him. "You're right. Maybe we'll both feel better if we do something. I need to go into Miles City to get groceries this morning. Why don't you come with me and we can pick up some paint."

"What color?" Maegan asked.

He could hear the hope in her voice. "I'm open to suggestions," he said.

"Maybe we should get some color charts and let Lilly chose. I think she's got quite an eye for color. Remember the work she did on Solomon's crown in Sunday school? It was lovely."

"She'll probably pick gold," Clint said, but the thought didn't bother him. He'd paint the whole house bubblegum-pink if it would make her stay. Suddenly, he wondered if she would have felt more at home with him if he'd painted her bedroom some girl color. And put up some ruffled white curtains. Instead, she'd stayed in Joe's old room with its tan walls and burlap curtains.

Maegan seemed to feel better by the time they hung up from their phone conversation, Clint thought. He knew he felt more hopeful. He might even get pink paint. What little girl could resist a princess bedroom? He wasn't going to just put up new curtains and paint. He was going to buy a new bedspread and rug and maybe even one of those sparkly rainbow makers that people put in windows. He should have realized when Lilly became so intent on beading that bridle that she liked pretty things.

He looked around at the kitchen after he hung up the phone. There would have to be changes here, too. He'd have to get out the tape measure before he headed into Dry Creek to pick up Maegan. If he could get curtains today, he would need to know the sizes of the windows in his house.

It wasn't until he was measuring his second window that he realized he would be reminded of Lilly every day from now on. Every wall would remind him of her. If she chose to leave anyway, that would be a whole lot of reminders of what he was missing.

It was too late though. Before Lilly, he had tried to protect himself by not being involved with people. But once he opened his heart to his niece, there was no going back.

The same was true with Maegan. Even though he had feelings for her, she would likely be leaving once she met Joe and assured herself that Lilly would be well-cared for by him. Oh, she'd be polite when she left.

He'd say he'd miss her. And she'd say they should keep in touch and he might even get a Christmas card from her. But his heart would never be the same. It wasn't just his house that would be changed forever; it would be him. He wasn't sure his solitude would be enough for him anymore.

Chapter Seven

It took three days for the paint to be delivered to the store in Miles City so it wasn't until Friday that Clint and Maegan started taking the lids off the cans in the upstairs of his house and flexing their brushes. The days had been blessedly dry so they could leave the windows at half-mast without worrying about rain. Still, even with the fresh air, the smell of paint was everywhere.

They had decided to start in Lilly's room.

"What's that?" Maegan said as she wrinkled her nose and pointed to something Clint had pushed out from under the bed as he swept.

He couldn't believe she could smell anything with the open cans of paint around, but then he looked closer at what he'd found. Maybe she couldn't exactly smell it, but she was anticipating the odor.

"I think it's one of Joe's old socks," Clint admitted as he squatted to take a better look. Surely he'd at least cleaned the room before he assigned it to Lilly. Although, come to think of it, he'd been calving when Joe brought the girl here and he was busy out in the barns. He knew he'd given her a set of clean sheets for the bed and he meant to go in and wash the windows and sort out the closet. He wasn't so sure he'd found time to do either though, since he'd had to mend that section of fence and then he'd moved the cattle to the pasture closer to the barn.

He shook his head. He had no excuse; he'd have to pay more attention to things from now on. He looked around. The only new thing Lilly had in her room was that teddy bear Maegan had given her. The girl had it propped up on a shelf beside Joe's collection of old junk. The poor bear was missing all of its beads and sparkles, but it didn't look any worse than some of the things Joe had left there a decade or two ago.

Then Clint noticed that Lilly had her porcelain dolls lined up on the shelf, too, with their pastel swirling skirts held out as though they were frozen in an everlasting ballroom dance. They were delicate and, now that he thought about it, those dolls were an odd match with

Lilly. She didn't seem the frilly sort and he'd never seen her even try to dance.

He glanced over and saw Maegan open the flaps on a box so she could fill it with the things from the shelf. They didn't want to get paint on any of it. He saw her reach for one of the dolls. "Where'd she get these?"

Clint shook his head. "The last I saw those dolls, she had them packed away in her suitcase. I don't know anything about them really."

Maegan brushed some dust off the closest one. "It'd be nice to have a pretty shelf just for them." Then she looked up. "Are you saying she brought these with her?"

Clint nodded. "I thought maybe she'd won them at a fair someplace."

The dolls were about four inches high and he hadn't noticed until now that they all had a bit of lavender in their dresses. It might just be on the sash or the bonnet, but the color was there on all of them. No wonder that was the color she'd chosen for her room.

"Keeping them in one piece when she was moving around to all those foster homes would have been difficult," Maegan muttered as she stared at them thoughtfully. "They must have been important to her."

"What did you lose?" Clint asked softly.

The sadness on her face told him some precious things had been broken or even taken from her.

Maegan looked at him and smiled. "I never felt I was like the other kids, not even the other ones in foster care. They didn't have a family. But I did—my sisters. It's just they were taken from me and no one would help me get them back."

"I would have helped," he said without thinking.

She blinked and he could see the tears in her eyes. "I know."

They were silent for a moment and Maegan turned her face away from him as though she didn't want him to see her tears.

Finally, Clint cleared his throat. He didn't want her to be uneasy around him. "I have a bit of wood in the barn that would make a nice shelf for Lilly," he said. "I can make it up in a few hours. Of course, the varnish will take longer, but it'll look a lot better than that shelf Joe had when he was a kid."

"I think she'd like that," Maegan said as she turned back to him.

His heart swelled a little just seeing that she was happier now. The shadows of her past would grow less over the years, he knew, because his had faded with God's help.

They just stood there and smiled at each other for a bit. The two of them had been doing that a lot lately. He figured she was more comfortable with him because they were on the same side now. He didn't want to examine his feelings too closely though. He was afraid his emotions went deeper than being allies or recognizing someone was on the same spiritual path as he was. He felt like a man on a precipice who was afraid to look over the edge for fear there was nothing but emptiness on the other side. He'd lived alone for so long, he wasn't sure a woman like Maegan would want to live with him now.

Still, he couldn't help but notice how cute she was with that red bandana wrapped around her head, her blond hair peeking out. Gradually, he realized the pink T-shirt and faded blue jeans she wore didn't look like any of the other clothes he'd seen her wear. And she'd been with him every day since Lilly announced she wanted to live with her father.

"You were thinking ahead. Packing paint clothes when you came," he said.

He was secretly glad that she didn't always look like an attorney. He was a rancher and there was nothing fancy about him.

"The clothes—oh, they belong to Doris

June, Mrs. Hargrove's daughter," Maegan admitted. "I'm afraid I didn't bring much in the way of clothes so I'm borrowing some."

"Well, they look real good on you."

"Thanks."

Clint thought she sounded surprised so he continued. "In fact, everything looks good on you. Very good."

He noticed her cheeks got rosy and he grinned. She didn't look at him though as she walked over and shook out the old blanket that had served as a bedspread. It was a khaki wool blanket left over from when his father was in the army. As family heirlooms went, this was the primary one for the Parkers. He wasn't sure he'd ever told Lilly that though. She probably just thought it was something from the rag bag.

"Lilly's going to like the comforter you bought her," Maegan said.

"I hope so. It was the only lavender one I could find and you know how she is about that color."

Maegan nodded ruefully. "Who would have thought she'd spend hours going over the color chart making sure she picked just the right shade?" Then she paused. "That's a good sign, isn't it? She wouldn't take that much time if she had already made a final and forever decision and knew she was going to leave, would she?"

"I don't know. I've asked myself all those questions, too," Clint said. "Worrying about it isn't going to make her stay though. We just need to keep working away."

"And praying," Maegan added softly.

"Yes, and praying," Clint agreed as he reached for his paintbrush. They all needed to talk to God about this. It was a good feeling to have someone by his side to pray with.

By the time they had to leave and meet Lilly, the walls of the girl's bedroom were light lavender. The door frames and the closet panels were deep lavender. White net curtains were ready to hang in the windows and Maegan had washed the new white sheets and made the bed with the pansy-flowered comforter.

"She's never going to leave this room," Maegan declared as she fluffed up the pillows on the bed. She couldn't remember when she'd felt so satisfied at the end of a job. She had already figured out that one of the reasons she was so determined to see Lilly happy was that she wanted to make up for some of the distress in her own childhood.

Still, that didn't make her longing wrong. She'd been meeting with Mrs. Hargrove every day to read the Bible and pray. One thing she'd learned was that God wanted her happiness. So, no, it wasn't wrong to want to be an involved aunt in Lilly's life. Or to ask God to bless her niece. And that niece's uncle.

"I'm never going to want to leave this room, either," Clint said as he folded up the metal stool he'd brought in to hang the curtain rods. "It makes the rest of the house look worn out."

"Well, we've got more paint." They had a can of yellow for the kitchen and an off-white one for the living room. Somewhere amidst the cans was even a peach color for the bathroom.

"Where's the paint for your room?" Maegan asked. She'd meant to ask earlier, but they'd gotten into a different discussion.

"Oh, Lilly's never in there," Clint said, dismissing the question as he picked up the stool and headed for the door.

"But—" Maegan protested. "You are and what if Lilly doesn't—"

Clint turned to look at her and she let her words trail off. She couldn't remind him that Lilly might not stay, that he might be living alone in this house. Besides, that wasn't really the point. "You deserve a nice room, too."

He turned and grunted at that. "I don't need anything fancy."

"It might be time for a change though," Maegan muttered as she followed him into the hall and down the stairs. One of the main things she had learned from her times with Mrs. Hargrove was that God wanted people to be willing to change—to give up their old patterns that were not working and try something new.

"Oh, I'm fine," he said again as he stopped at the bottom of the chair and looked around. "This old house never was much of a showcase."

Maegan could see that for herself. The sofa had a brown blanket thrown over it and a metal trunk stood in for a coffee table. The windows were wide and the view outside was stunning, but the curtains were too short and faded to do any of it justice. "If it's money, I—"

"Oh, there's plenty of money," Clint protested. "I've had some good years recently. The bank account is almost fat."

"I was going to say I could make some curtains," Maegan continued. "I sew pretty well and drapes are not that hard to do."

She had to admit it was a bold offer. Most

men didn't want a woman decorating their house. "I mean, since we're painting some of the rooms anyway. You could pick out the fabric, of course."

Clint looked around again. "I guess a new paint job will make the rest of the house look pretty shabby unless I do something. But I wouldn't want to take your time. Or I could pay you. I hate to let you use all your vacation time unless I pay you. That way it won't be so bad that you're not working."

Maegan hesitated. She hadn't told him the latest. "Actually, my job called and they have me working on some projects while I'm here."

"Really?"

She nodded. "I made a lot of connections in the social services area when I was looking for my sisters. Turns out some groups on the internet found out about what I did—these are people who want to find their families, too—and they called the law firm I work for and they got me started on it."

"And you can do it all from here?" Clint asked intently, an odd note of something she couldn't identify in his voice.

"Pretty much. It's phone work mostly. I

called around for an hour or so before I came out here this morning."

Clint nodded in seeming satisfaction. "That's good. Real good. I— Well, that's good is all. I—"

Maegan had never seen Clint stammer before. She hadn't thought he was the type to fumble anything. Now, he might refuse to answer something. She'd encountered that a few times in the days they'd spent together. And sometimes he said something was okay when it clearly wasn't. He'd rather suffer than complain. But she'd never seen him choke on his words before.

"I'm not going to charge you for the curtains," Maegan finally said. That was the only thing she could think of that might be giving him trouble.

He shook his head like that wasn't where his mind had gone. "I'm just glad you can work from Dry Creek. That's all."

"Oh, yeah, that should work out fine for now," she said.

Clint stood there, facing her and ignoring the questions in her eyes. He needed to get the knots out of his tongue before she thought he'd gone daft. He'd almost stepped over that precipice without even thinking about it.

He'd been going to say that maybe she could have a job in Dry Creek long-term. He might have even asked about them having a future together.

He was a fool sometimes, but he hoped he had enough sense to know that a woman like Maegan didn't make a snap judgment when it came to her future. They'd known each other a week now. People didn't fall in love in that little time, did they?

When he didn't say anything, Maegan looked at her watch.

"Shouldn't we go get Lilly?" she asked and the moment was gone.

Clint thought he'd be relieved. He'd avoided the plunge into embarrassment. But it didn't feel as good as he thought it would.

Of course, Maegan was right. It was time to head into town and get Lilly.

Clint had picked Maegan up when he'd taken Lilly to the bus this morning so they both rode in his pickup to meet the bus at the café.

The gravel road leading into town was packed solid now that the rain had stopped. The sun had been bright for most of the day, but it was still chilly. Maegan was quiet for most of the ride and Clint had let his cautious nature guide him.

Driving into the small town of Dry Creek though, he remembered other times—all those times as a boy when he hadn't reached out and asked someone to help him and Joe have a better life. He knew the town here didn't look like much, but people took risks every day. The old men who gathered in the hardware store could swap tales about times when they planted crops that had been wiped out by drought or hordes of grasshoppers. They'd suffered loss. But he knew that, if he asked them, they'd tell him there were times in a man's life when he needed to risk everything on the chance that he would find something precious.

Clint pulled his pickup to a stop near the café and looked over at Maegan. A strand of her hair was escaping the bandana she still wore. She had a smudge of lavender paint on her cheekbone. She had none of the makeup she'd worn when they first met and she looked tired. Yet, she was more beautiful than he had ever seen her.

All of a sudden the precipice he thought he was facing turned into a gentle hillside, the kind he used to roll down as a boy. Those times had been refreshing and sweet. He reached out and tucked Maegan's hair behind her bandana. He left his thumb there, resting on her cheek. She was so still he thought he could feel her pulse.

And then she looked up at him. Her eyes shimmered with emotions. He didn't suppose she liked being shut out any more than he would have liked it if she was holding back.

He smiled and softly moved his thumb down her cheek until he rested it beneath her chin. "What I meant to say earlier was that I would like it very much if you came to live here in Dry Creek. I know the job might take some doing, but people here have legal problems, too. Between that and the work you're getting from your current firm, you could have a practice."

She blinked and he knew he couldn't stop there. "It's about you and me, too. I want us to have a future together." He could feel her pulse quicken. "I don't want to pressure you. There's nothing to worry about. I just want you to know the thought of being with you doesn't make me worry that I'm jumping off a cliff."

She blinked again and her eyes crinkled with amusement. Her pulse steadied and she put her hand up to his to hold it in place.

"I thought you might be afraid of heights," she said solemnly.

"Now how would you know that?" he asked, content now that she was curving her face into the palm of his hand.

"Because I'm scared of heights, too," she whispered.

"Well," he said. "We'd make quite the pair then, wouldn't we?"

He felt her nod with her head against his hand. He curled his hand under her chin and tipped her face up slightly so he could bend down and kiss her. The first one was quick and much too fleeting. But as he angled his head to kiss again, he heard his heart start to pound in an alarming way. He stopped and realized it wasn't his heart that he was hearing.

He turned his head and saw that Lilly was knocking on the window of his pickup. He saw the bus in the background and the other children running to other cars. He and Maegan had been in lost in their own world. He glanced over at her and saw she was adjusting her hair.

"The window," she whispered at him.

He opened the door instead. Lilly was standing there with her backpack slung over her shoulder. "We were just—" he tried to think "—I mean, we were waiting for you and—"

"Please," Lilly said as she rolled her eyes. "I've seen kissing before."

"Oh, yes, I suppose." Clint wondered what the rules were for foster parents. He pulled his seat forward so she could slip into the backseat of his pickup.

"My dad kisses women all the time," Lilly declared with indifference as she threw her backpack inside and slid in.

Clint frowned slightly as he turned to face the girl. "I really don't think you ought to be—"

Lilly was getting a belligerent look on her face.

"We finished painting your room today," Maegan interrupted with cheer in her voice.

Clint realized that now wasn't the time to question Lilly on the morals of her father. Besides, he didn't need to ask her much. He knew his brother. That's why he'd devised a proposition for Joe that the man wouldn't turn down.

"Is it lavender?" Lilly asked, not quite relaxing yet. "Did it come out looking like the color it's supposed to be?"

"It's perfect," Maegan assured her.

The smile on Lilly's face made Clint content. He wished he'd taken out a paintbrush when the girl first came to his house. He'd do anything to see that the girl was happy. He hadn't told anyone yet, but he'd figured out what he could do for Lilly. He was going to offer the ranch to Joe in exchange for him raising Lilly. He had already bought Joe's portion of the ranch from him ten years ago, but Joe might be ready to settle down and he liked owning things.

Unfortunately, if he gave his brother all of his money, he would be starting over himself. He knew a couple of jobs that were open in Dry Creek and he'd get by. He figured it would sour his chances with Maegan, but he was going to ask her to be his wife anyway when everything was settled with the girl. If a man couldn't risk his pride for love, then he was a poor man indeed.

Clint started the pickup again and backed out of the spot where he'd parked. Maegan was going to have dinner with them tonight and then he was going to drive her back to her room over Mrs. Hargrove's garage. They all had a routine these days and it was one that satisfied him. It was five more days until his brother's birthday and he'd called Joe yesterday reminding him he was expected for dinner that night. Lilly planned to make him a chocolate cake with candles and Maegan promised to make a chicken enchilada recipe that Mrs. Hargrove had shown her.

Clint planned to call his brother on Monday and remind him again. As bad as it would hurt to have Lilly ask to go with Joe, he could deal with that better than the hurt Lilly would feel if his brother didn't bother to show up. That's why Clint was going to drop a hint or two that there was money involved for Joe. Significant money. That would bring his brother running.

Chapter Eight

Maegan lay in bed the morning of Joe Parker's birthday and wondered if the promised thundershowers were going to come this morning. She didn't need to look out the windows to see everything was unusually dark. Besides, the air felt heavy and the glass in the windows appeared damp. She should be getting up, but she didn't want to move. She was trying hard not to be depressed.

Then, again, why should she bother being happy? Clint had finally told her that he was planning to offer his brother money to raise Lilly, on the condition that he would move to the ranch so Clint could keep an eye on the girl. At first, Maegan thought the idea had some merit. But then Clint explained he would probably not be living on the ranch with Joe and Lilly; he didn't think his brother would compromise that much. Besides, the ranch would be the bulk of the payment to Joe.

Instead, Clint would rent a place in Dry Creek. When he said that, she expected him to make some remark about her moving to the small town, too. But he didn't. So she assumed he'd decided they had no future together. Of course, he'd probably expect her to visit Lilly sometimes, but that would be the end of it. The thought of a string of Christmas cards tying her to Clint and Lilly, year after year, seemed almost worse than no contact at all.

Almost, but not quite. In her deepest heart, she knew she'd take whatever scraps she was allowed. She had never come so close to having her dreams come true and that made seeing them crumble hard. But she still wanted whatever she could get. Her new Bible, a gift from Mrs. Hargrove, was sitting on the stand beside her bed and Maegan knew she only had to start to read its pages to feel her sorrows ease. Somehow, in all of this, God had a purpose.

So, she swung her legs around to the side of the bed and stretched her arms high. First, she would be thankful that God had blessed her with a niece like Lilly. Even if she wouldn't be able to spend much time with her, she

could pray for the girl throughout the years
and maybe she would grow into a faithful
woman of God. That was no small thing.

In the meantime, Maegan had cheese to
grate and refried beans to cook. She was helping Lilly make a Mexican meal for her father
and she insisted everything be ready for her to
finish by the time she came home from school
today. They'd baked the chocolate cake last
night so it was ready to frost. Mrs. Hargrove
was sending over some homemade flan and
Maegan had bought a small can of chilies
to put in the enchiladas and the beans. Clint
claimed he could make a good Mexican rice
so he was in charge of that. The rest was in
Lilly's hands.

Fortunately, Maegan thought, the paint had
dried in the living room and yesterday she and
Clint had driven to Billings to get a whole
box of Mexican-themed decorations. The bold
red-and-black stripes of some blankets they'd
also bought would make the white room look
festive.

If Joe didn't fall down in astonishment at all
the trouble his daughter had gone to—that all
of them had gone to—Maegan figured she'd
be entitled to have some words with the man,
somewhere in private so she didn't have to
watch her tongue. She had no doubts that the

man was used to getting what he wanted in life. He was a charmer from all she'd heard. But he didn't know who he was up against if he thought she would give him a pass on manners. Especially not today.

Clint came to pick her up after he'd delivered Lilly to the bus. The two of them had fallen into the habit of going back to the café and having a cup of coffee or tea once Lilly was off to school, but they didn't today. It wasn't just that they had a lot to do. Things had been strained between them for the past few days.

"I found the cast iron kettle I told you about," Clint said as he backed his pickup out of the driveway where she'd met him. "It cleaned up nice."

The sky was still overcast and the road was slightly muddy. She'd set the covered dish of flan on the floorboard before she climbed into the pickup. Now, she bent down and moved it to the seat. "It's going to be quite the party."

Clint grunted.

She glanced sideways at him and tried to read his face. He didn't seem as upset as she had expected, but she knew he didn't always talk about what was bothering him. There was no betraying tightness to his lips or strained muscle in his jaw though. His eyes were looking straight ahead, and she didn't think they'd show any distress.

"I got a few last-minute tips from Mrs. Hargrove for the enchiladas," she said as the pickup left the small town.

It was silent for a moment and then he cleared his throat. "Lilly asked me if I had a present for her father." Clint glanced over at her. "I'm planning to give him everything I have and she wants a present."

"The ranch is—"

"I meant Lilly—she's the everything," he interrupted gruffly and looked over at Maegan a little ruefully. "I had this fantasy going about Lilly and me living on the ranch and then you came and I thought all of us—" He stopped.

She noticed his knuckles were white where they gripped the steering wheel. She waited for him to continue with what he was saying, but he was silent. Maybe it was for the best. She suspected he wasn't exactly thinking they would be together now, either with Lilly or without her.

"Have you made Joe your offer yet?" she asked.

He nodded. "He's thinking about it."

"What will you do if he decides to take the ranch?"

"They need some help at the Elkton place.

And, if that doesn't work out there, I can drive into Miles City and find something. They always need help at the grocery store."

The thought of Clint selling deli meats or stacking cans didn't seem right. "Surely, your brother can't expect to take it all."

"You don't know Joe. Besides, he was making noise about some woman he's met. He might be ready to settle down. He'll need money to do that."

The drizzle that had been coming down turned to steady rain. Clint turned on the windshield wipers and the steady rhythm they made filled the cab.

"Don't worry," Clint finally said. "It won't take long for me to get on my feet again. I might even be able to save enough to make a down payment on another ranch."

He said the last part in the hearty way people did when they knew it wasn't likely.

"I hope you do," Maegan said softly.

They rode the rest of the way to the ranch just listening to the rain.

By six o'clock that night, Clint had put on his white shirt and pulled the lace tablecloth down from the upstairs closet. He'd even rooted around until he found a white candle on the back of a closet shelf. Lilly had been home from school for over two hours and his brother should have pulled in thirty minutes ago. The sun had already set and there were no lights coming down the road.

"He probably just had some trouble with the traffic," Maegan was telling the girl as they turned down the heat in the oven. She hadn't bothered to say where Joe might have run into a bottleneck of cars. "He'll be here soon, I'm sure."

Maegan looked up as Clint came into the kitchen and he saw the frustration in her eyes. She clearly knew there was no traffic. They had worried all day and Joe hadn't bothered to be on time. The table was all set and Lilly had put a wrapped box on Joe's chair. Clint had even bought the lavender paper for the present.

"I'll call his cell phone," Clint said. Joe didn't always answer, he thought, but it was the best they could do.

Just then he heard the sound of a vehicle coming down the road.

"He's here," Lilly screamed as she ran to the window to check. It was almost dark outside, but she stood there for a moment, the wild excitement on her face a thing of beauty. Then she turned around. "It must be him. He's really here. Remember, we're going to sing

'Happy Birthday' right when he comes in the door," the girl admonished Clint and Maegan, her hands fluttering over everything. She had stepped away from the window and had moved over to the table. "Don't let him see us yet. We won't light the candles, but—"

Clint felt his jaw clench. He hoped he had impressed upon his brother the need to be nice tonight. Lilly was so excited and Joe so unpredictable.

A knock sounded from the back door and Lilly looked to him and whispered, "Answer it, please."

Clint nodded and walked over, reaching for the knob. The porch light was on, but even if it hadn't been he would have recognized the face of his brother as he stood there looking sheepish. What he hadn't expected to see in the circle of light was a young woman, dark-haired and statuesque. Joe had his arm around her.

"Happy—" Clint heard Lilly's thin voice begin to sing and then stop. By then, the door had opened wide enough that everyone could see the two people standing on the porch.

Everyone was silent for a moment.

"Sorry we're late," Joe finally said as he ushered the woman through the doorway and stepped into the house himself.

Clint nodded as he stepped back to give his brother some room.

It was awkward as everyone just looked at each other.

"You're probably wondering about my sweet Carina here," Joe finally said, with a smile at the woman. "I thought it was time she met my family before it was too late to make a difference."

Clint turned to the woman and bowed his head slightly. "Welcome, Carina."

The woman smiled her greeting in return and Clint formally introduced Maegan. Then the silence stretched for longer than it should.

Finally, Maegan spoke. "Well, dinner is ready. Why don't you take your coats off so you can be comfortable?"

No one lit the candle in the middle of the table. While Joe and Carina were in the living room, hanging their coats in the closet there, Lilly moved the balloons away from the table.

"I'm sorry," Maegan whispered as she put her hand on the girl's shoulder. Clint had gone into the living room with his brother, and left her and Lilly in the kitchen to put the food on the table.

"Who is she anyway?" Lilly grumbled in disappointment.

Maegan had no answer to the question so she started pulling the dish of enchiladas out of the oven. After that, she took out the refried beans and the rice. The lettuce salad was in the refrigerator and the salsa was already on the table.

The dinner conversation was awkward. Joe seemed impatient with the prayer Clint offered and his friend, Carina, didn't say a word about anything. Instead, she would turn her shimmering brown eyes on each speaker and smile politely. They were half through the meal when Joe casually mentioned that she didn't speak English.

"I met Carina in Brazil," he added.

Maegan relaxed at that. If the woman had been visiting Joe, she could understand why he had to bring her to dinner. He could hardly leave her alone in whatever rodeo town he was in. Maegan looked over and met Clint's eyes. By his expression, she could tell he'd come to the same conclusion.

Lilly wasn't as easily satisfied though.

"When does she go back?" the girl asked.

Joe gave a nervous laugh. "We'll talk about that later."

Maegan felt like she was getting a headache. Why would they need to talk about anything later? The man's daughter was asking for some simple reassurance.

Apparently, Lilly mellowed though because, when they had finished eating, she brought out the matches to light the candles on the cake. Maegan got up and brought the cake back from the refrigerator.

Joe seemed to like the candles and asked for a large slice of the chocolate cake, winking at Lilly.

"You know what I like," he added and gave the girl a quick kiss on the top of her head. Lilly beamed.

The girl waited for everyone to finish their cake. Then she reached behind her chair and brought out the package for him to open.

Maegan's heart sank when Joe accepted the gift with a smile and then handed it to Carina to open for him.

Clint started to say something, but Joe cut him off. "Carina has those nails. They slice right through tape."

"Lilly worked very hard on her gift," Clint warned him.

Maegan prayed. She didn't even really know what to pray for, she just knew this was an important moment for Lilly and so much could go wrong.

"Lilly's a worker, all right," Joe said with pride.

Carina reached out and held the opened box for Joe to see. Maegan held her breath as the man held up the bridle and examined it.

"Nice," Joe said in a neutral tone. "Very nice."

"Lilly looked all over for the beads," Clint offered pointedly.

Joe nodded as he set the bridle back in the box.

Maegan suddenly realized the man hadn't made eye contact with Lilly since he came in the door. He had patted her on the head and talked to her, but he hadn't met her gaze. And, it was hard to avoid doing so because the girl had her eyes trained on him most of the time.

"Maybe Lilly would like to show you her room," Maegan suggested. The girl had said earlier she wanted to do that. Maybe the two of them just needed some time alone to get comfortable with one another again. Then when Joe looked at his friend, Maegan added quickly, "I can entertain Carina. There's so much I'd like to know about Brazil."

Fortunately, no one pointed out the obvious,

that Carina couldn't speak English and Maegan couldn't speak Portuguese. Instead, Joe stood up and gestured for Lilly to lead the way.

Maegan waited to hear footsteps on the stairway up to the second floor before she leaned over to Clint and said, "It's going okay, don't you think? I mean once we got over the initial greetings and all."

He nodded. "I hope so."

He didn't look convinced and she didn't want to press him for reassurance. Things of the heart often took time and maybe Joe needed to understand Lilly better and see how much she loved him. What man's heart wouldn't melt in front of the fierce loyalty of Lilly?

Maegan turned to Carina and smiled. She gestured to the necklace the woman was wearing and tried to tell her with gestures how lovely she thought it was. Carina reciprocated by moving her hands to indicate she admired Maegan's hair. Friendships had been built on less, Maegan thought, and then she saw the ring.

"Oh," she gasped and looked over at Clint. She knew Carina didn't know English, but it still seemed impolite to say aloud that she was surprised to see a wedding ring on the woman's finger.

"She must be his wife," Clint guessed, his voice devoid of emotion. "I— Maybe that's good." He looked over at Maegan. "For Lilly's sake."

Maegan had to think about that for a minute or two. She supposed it was better for Lilly to have two parents, but Carina couldn't even speak English. How would the two communicate? And the way Joe had handled the introduction made Lilly resent the woman.

About then, she heard a strong set of footsteps coming down the stairs. It was Joe. Maegan looked behind him, expecting to see Lilly any minute but only the man stood there.

"Could I talk with you a minute?" Joe said to Clint. "Out on the porch?"

Clint nodded as he stood up. "I've been expecting to talk."

After the two men walked out the kitchen door, Maegan looked over at Carina. "Excuse me a minute."

The other woman nodded as though she understood.

That was all the permission Maegan needed. She hurried to the stairs. She had a feeling something had gone wrong. She felt another wordless prayer beating through her as she took each step as fast as she could.

Lilly was sitting on her bed, her dolls spread around her. She looked up when Maegan stood in the doorway.

"May I come in?" Maegan asked.

The girl nodded. Her face was pale and her shoulders slumped.

The two sat in silence for a minute before Maegan asked, "Is something wrong?"

Lilly looked up at her and the bleakness on her face tore at Maegan's heart.

Eventually, the girl said, "He didn't know about the dolls." She paused to swallow. "My mother told me he had sent the dolls to me for my birthdays. Every birthday I got one of these dolls in a beautiful box. It was supposed to show he loved me, that I was his little girl. My mom promised me he loved me."

A single sob ripped through the girl and Maegan took her in her arms and held her.

"I'm so sorry. So very sorry," Maegan murmured.

"I kept them in my suitcase and didn't show them to anyone," Lilly continued, tears streaming freely down her face. "I was waiting to show them to him when we had a home—just the two of us."

Maegan rocked the girl. "I know, sweetheart. I know."

"My mother said he loved me more than anyone in the world," Lilly said, her confusion plain as she looked up.

"He doesn't love you more than your Uncle Clint," Maegan assured her.

Tears flowed from both of them at that.

It was a half hour before they walked back downstairs. The house felt empty and someone had put away the leftovers, stacking the dishes in the sink.

"My dad forgot his bridle," Lilly said as she stepped farther into the kitchen.

Maegan saw that the box had been slid halfway under one of the chairs. The beads in the bridle shone as bright as they had earlier, but she could hardly look at them. "Maybe he's just outside. In the barn or somewhere."

As soon as she said the words, Maegan knew they were not true. She couldn't imagine Carina looking at cattle. Besides, Clint would never take his brother there, not when Lilly had been so determined to spend every second she could with the man.

Just then Clint opened the door and came

inside the kitchen from the porch. He looked at them both.

"My dad's gone, isn't he?" Lilly stated with more composure than Maegan felt.

"I'm afraid so," Clint said, a note of helplessness in his voice.

They were all silent for a few minutes. Finally Clint added in a flat voice, "He told me to tell you goodbye. I tried to get him to go upstairs and tell you himself, but he refused and—" Clint spread his hands. Maegan saw his knuckles were scraped so she knew the refusal had been contested. "Anyway, he's going back to Brazil. It seems his wife has some property down there and—well, he's going to live there now." Sheer defeat sounded in Clint's voice. "I'm sorry."

"That's okay," Lilly said, her voice small. "He wasn't the father I thought he was anyway."

And, with that, she walked slowly over to Clint and wrapped her arms around his waist.

"Can I stay with you?" she asked.

Maegan saw him blink back a tear as he said, "Always."

She wasn't sure if it was Clint or Lilly who

opened the hug and gestured for her to join them. Either way, she went with hope in her heart. Clint had his arm around her and he turned slightly so they could kiss over Lilly's head.

The first kiss was tentative. But Maegan felt the warmth of the second kiss slide all the way down to her toes.

"I'm going to ask you to marry me, you know," Clint whispered in her ear a little later. "I figure I need to wait a few more days so we will have known each other for two weeks. I don't want us to look impulsive."

"That would never do," Maegan agreed with a smile. She would enjoy saying yes to this man.

Lilly stepped away from them a bit. "Does this mean we're all going to live together?" she asked, a note of wonder in her words. "In the same house?"

Clint nodded. "If Maegan agrees."

"Please," Lilly said as she looked up at her.

Maegan nodded, her eyes on Clint. "I'd love to be part of this family."

Clint's arm tightened around her and he kissed her again. They stood there together for a long time. This, Maegan thought with satisfaction as she looked at both Lilly and

Clint, was finally the family she had been dreaming of for years.

"I love you," Clint whispered to Maegan.

"I love you, too," she answered him and then looked down to meet Lilly's eyes. "I'm so glad I've found my family at last."

* * * * *

QUESTIONS FOR DISCUSSION

1. In *A Dry Creek Family,* Maegan Shay is working hard to find the last members of her family. She is unwilling to accept a substitute family if she can't have her biological family. Have you ever felt like she does? That, even though something is logical, it doesn't work for you because of your feelings? Tell us about it.

2. As a child, Maegan prayed for God to give her adoptive parents who were willing to take her and her sisters. When He didn't give her that, she gave up on Him. Many of us have given up on God at some point in our lives. Has that been your experience? What happened?

3. If you could have sat down with Maegan at that point (see question 2), what would you have told her about God? Are there any Bible verses you would have showed her?

4. Clint Parker accepts his niece at his ranch because he believes his brother will return the girl to social services if he doesn't.

Clint is a reluctant parent, but he believes God wants him to do what he can for Lilly. Have you ever accepted a responsibility that belongs to someone else? How did it make you feel?

5. It was also difficult for Clint to stand in for his brother as Lilly's guardian because the girl clearly idolized her father and was cool toward Clint. It's easy for children to take their parents for granted, just like Lilly took her uncle for granted. Do you take people in your family for granted? Do you have any suggestions for how to change this?

6. Mrs. Hargrove is the one who helps Maegan see things clearly. Do you have someone like Mrs. Hargrove in your life? Are you a Mrs. Hargrove to someone else?

A MOTHER
FOR MULE HOLLOW

Debra Clopton

This book is dedicated to
my wonderful church family
at Faith Baptist Church in Madisonville, Texas.

Casting all your care upon Him,
for He cares for you.
—1 *Peter* 5:7

Chapter One

"I asked you not to come."

Olivia Dancer wasn't exactly certain how to take Gabe McKennon's words. Or the staunch stance he'd taken the instant he'd opened the door to his home and found her standing on the porch. He'd planted his jean-clad legs wide, his scuffed boots anchoring him in the threshold like solid timber, as he crossed his arms and scowled down at her.

She didn't like the look at all. "Your mother invited me." Her words were defensive, meeting his cerulean-blue eyes with a challenge of her own. The rugged cowboy's jaw stiffened beneath his dark five o'clock shadow and his eyes narrowed. The man had a problem but Olivia stood her ground, though she was confused by his attitude. He looked like he was about to explode beneath his Stetson.

"My mother *invited* you?"

"Yes. She called last week and invited us out here. She said you had come to your senses—her words not mine."

His jaw jerked again. Temper, temper, Olivia wanted to say but didn't. She had been perplexed by his attitude a few weeks earlier when she'd called him to meet her nephew and he'd refused. She was growing more and more concerned by the minute.

Why would he tell her he didn't want her to come to town to meet her nephew—whom she'd just learned existed a few weeks ago?

"My mother needs to learn her boundaries."

The man was digging in deeper and deeper on the not-so-likeable scale. "All she did was tell me you'd thought about the situation and changed your mind. That you both would be happy for me and my daughter to come meet Wesley. Obviously something was lost over the phone line."

"Obviously," he grunted. "And his name is Wes."

"Wes, I'm sorry. The birth papers said Wesley."

"Mom," Trudy, her ten-year-old daughter, called from the truck. "Can I pul-eeze get out of this truck?"

Olivia shot her a warning glance. "No, Trudy. Stay put."

"But Mom—"

"Trudy!"

"Yes, ma'am," Trudy huffed in exasperation at the tone of Olivia's voice. Flouncing back she hunkered down in the seat, the top of her head barely visible over the dashboard. Her attitude had not been good since Olivia had made the decision to drive from Houston to Mule Hollow. But then, Trudy had had trouble processing change ever since her daddy's death three years ago. Justin's death had been hard on everyone who'd loved him, but particularly his little girl.

"Look," Olivia said, refocusing on Disgruntled Cowboy. "I don't know what your mother was thinking. You're making it clear that you are not okay with us being here."

One straight brown eyebrow quirked downward in a "ya-think?" attitude. "My mother and I disagree on the issue."

"Again, that's pretty clear," Olivia drawled, her thick Texas twang enhanced by her temper as it began to percolate at his entire stance. "Who do you think you are anyway? Your son is the son of my deceased sister. A sister that I've just realized I had." The last few months had been surprising, shocking and wonderful in that she'd learned she had two sisters she'd been separated from when she was very young. Maegan, her older sister, was alive and well, and they were getting to know each other after all these years. But they'd searched for their younger sister and recently found that she'd died three years ago.

She'd been saddened by the news and hurt through and through thinking about how their lives had been ripped apart, and they'd never, ever get to meet—at least here on earth. Maegan and Olivia's only consolation was learning that Dawn, their deceased sister, had children.

Wes was her four-year-old son. She also had a daughter by another man. Olivia and Maegan had decided they should go and check on Dawn's children. Maegan had gone to Montana to see about Dawn's little girl who was living with a single uncle. To her total surprise Maegan and Clint Parker had fallen in love! Olivia was still in shock about that. It had happened so quickly. Why, it had happened before she'd even been able to get her life lined out in order to make the trip to Mule Hollow.

Gabe McKennon hadn't wanted her to come. "With or without your mother's invitation I was coming out here. I have a right and a duty to meet my nephew and to make absolutely certain that he is being well cared for." She didn't add that Gabe McKennon was not helping satisfy her mind.

"I'm Wes's dad, and he is being well cared for. I do what I believe is best for him."

"And meeting his aunt is bad?" Why would he not want her around—what was bad about that? What was he hiding? "Look, I have a right to meet my nephew." Staring at him she set her own stubborn jaw. "Is your mother here? Is Wes here?"

"No."

That did it. "Look, Mr. McKennon. I am going to meet my nephew whether you want me to or not. It is my right. I'm going to see for myself that he is happy and doing well."

The irritating man's brows flattened, and a crease formed between them. "I can assure you he is both."

"Excuse me if I insist that I need my own assurances, thank you very much. Your attitude so far hasn't eased my mind." There was no sense beating around the bush. She'd given him the courtesy of a phone call in the beginning and he'd given her nothing. "What kind of dad are you anyway?" One thing was certain—she wasn't leaving town until she found out.

"My attitude is concern for my son. I'm sorry if you feel put out, but I'm Wes's dad, and my job is to keep him healthy. And that means being cautious about the people I let into his life."

Of all the insulting... Olivia had just been told she wasn't good enough to be in her nephew's life! This would not do. Not do at all.

Gabe was going to have to have a serious talk with his mother. It wasn't like her to go against his wishes on something as serious as Wes's well-being. He'd been startled three weeks earlier when he'd been contacted by his ex-wife's sisters. He hadn't known Dawn had sisters or that she'd been adopted as a baby. There was a lot he hadn't known about Dawn. But the moment he'd opened the door and laid eyes on Olivia Dancer, there was absolutely no denying who she was. Olivia resembled Dawn, and there was no denying that they were sisters. They had the same heart-shaped face, with lively, amber eyes that were tilted up at the edges.

Behind him he heard the back door open and his stomach clenched. Whether he'd wanted this meeting or not, unless he did something quick, it was about to happen. His mother and Wes's happy chatter filled the rooms behind him as they came in from picking tomatoes in the garden. Wes loved to garden. Wes loved everything.

"He doesn't know about you," Gabe snapped, feeling roped and tied. This was a nightmare. The mother of his son abandoned them the second the baby was born. She'd taken her small daughter he'd grown attached to and told him she wanted him to leave them alone. It had all been tough to deal with. Now her sister wanted to insinuate herself into the life of his son. And his own *mother* instigated the situation behind his back. What was she thinking? Gabe scowled. It was pretty obvious mothers stuck together...and tossed their sons under the bull. He didn't like it. Not one bit.

At the sound of Wes's voice Olivia's eyes brightened.

"Mom," her daughter called from the truck. "Can I pul-leeze get out?"

"No, stay in the truck," she called to her daughter and then turned back to him. "Is that Wes?"

Gabe heard his mother's approaching footsteps and felt himself sinking in quicksand. Wes was chattering away about a "whopper of a tomato." As if he were in the middle of a collision course, Gabe could only stand there. He was a man who could make split decisions in a matter of seconds, but suddenly looking at the bright, expectant eyes of Olivia Dancer, he hesitated. That hesitation cost him—it gave his mother time to make it to him before he could shut the door. What had he planned to do anyway—pretend Olivia hadn't come by? Not a very diplomatic remedy to the problem. Then again, where Wes was concerned, he wasn't worried about diplomacy, he was worried about his son. Thankfully he heard his mother send Wes to wash his hands, which gave Gabe a few seconds to get this situation turned around.

"Gabe, who is at the door?"

Gabe glared at Olivia, wanting more than anything to close the door on her. He almost did, but even he thought that was too rude.

Holding his ground in front of the door, he glanced over his shoulder at his barely five-foot mother. "*Georgetta,* we need to talk."

Chapter Two

Georgetta McKennon cocked her sandy-blond head to the side and eyed Gabe suspiciously. She was alert since she knew he only called her Georgetta when he was really unhappy about something she'd done.

"*Gabe*, are you going to step out of the way and let me see who you're hiding on the other side of that door?"

He was looking over his shoulder at her, blocking her vision, though he knew it was a losing battle. His mother wasn't much bigger than a powder keg but just as explosive as they came. "I'd rather not," he grunted. "But since you're responsible for her being here, I guess I have no choice."

His mother's eyes lit with enthusiasm, and she clapped her hands together. "Wonderful! Olivia is here," she gushed—actually gushed—as she swept past him. She proceeded to completely ignore his bad mood by greeting Olivia like she was her long-lost best friend.

"What a pleasure to have you here." Pink with excitement, Georgetta bypassed a handshake and wrapped her arms around the woman. "This is wonderful. Just wonderful!"

Looking a bit overwhelmed, Olivia stepped back, smiling warmly. "I'm glad to be here."

The genuineness of her smile hit him in the gut, and instantly Gabe felt his hope sinking—no way was he going to get his way here. Nope…his mother had taken sides against him in this situation, and that wasn't good. It was also wholly unexpected.

"I've got your rooms ready, and we are so excited you are here to stay with us for a few weeks."

"Rooms? Stay!" Gabe rambled as his temper shot up. *"Weeks."* His mother had been busier than he realized—how could she have invited Olivia and her daughter to spend a few weeks with them on his ranch—in his house? "She isn't staying here."

He put his foot down.

"Yes, she is."

"Mother. *Georgetta*—"

Georgetta cut him off with an exasperated

look. He'd received that look many times growing up. It was the "I've-taught-you-better-than-that" look.

"It's okay," Olivia interjected, giving him a glare of her own. "We can stay in town."

Good. He'd rather her not stay at all—but staying in Mule Hollow was better than nothing.

"You will do no such thing." Georgetta shot him a stern look. "This house is plenty big, and I invited you. You are my guests." She pointed toward Olivia's truck. "*You,* grab Olivia's suitcases," she ordered Gabe. To Olivia she spoke softer. "Let's get Trudy out of that truck. Wes will be out any minute—"

"You will say nothing to Wes about this. And you won't, either," he demanded to Olivia.

"I wouldn't think of saying anything to hurt Wesley—Wes," she corrected. "But surely he knows about his mother."

Georgetta gave a quick nod. "He knows about her, but he never knew her. She—"

"She didn't hang around long enough to hold him at the hospital." Gabe had no forgiveness in his heart for Dawn. She'd been tired of pretending that she had any kind of love in her heart by the sixth month, and when the baby was born she'd refused to even look at Wes. How did a woman not look at her son?

Olivia's eyes widened. "She didn't hold him? I don't understand."

"Join the club."

"That's enough, Gabe. Olivia, we'll talk about this more later." Trudy had gotten out of the truck and was walking up the steps. She didn't look any more thrilled at being here than he was that they were here.

The girl resembled Wes if Gabe looked hard enough. They had the same face shape, same eyes. Except Trudy looked guarded right now. Or just plain uncomfortable like him.

"Trudy," Olivia said. "This is Georgetta and Gabe McKennon."

"Hello," Georgetta said, totally enthralled with the situation that she ignored the clear signs of trouble here. "I'm so excited that Wes has a cousin! You are lovely. How old are you?"

Trudy's gaze slid from Gabe's mother to him, pausing on him before she looked down. "I'm ten."

Olivia placed her arm around Trudy's shoulders. "She just had a birthday."

"I'm sure that was fun." Georgetta smiled.

Gabe listened and tried to process the fact that these strangers were supposed to be staying in his home. His mother lived here, too, and had a right to invite whomever she wanted to stay. But still... Wes strode out of the house, breaking into Gabe's thoughts. His son gave a wide smile the instant he saw Olivia and Trudy. Gabe felt the situation tilting their way.

"Hi," Wes said, older than his four years. "I don't know you."

Olivia chuckled, bent down and held out her hand. "I'm Olivia and this is my daughter, Trudy."

"I'm Wes McKennon." He shook their hands, beaming—Wes was a friendly little guy and had never met a stranger. Gabe felt his heart twist with love and pride at how he proclaimed who he was. This was his son. He loved him more than anything. "I've got a horse. You want to see him?" he asked Trudy, who looked startled but nodded.

"That's a great idea," Georgetta said. "I'll take the children to look at Pony Boy. You two can get better acquainted, and you can show Olivia where the guest rooms are."

It was a clear day in May, but Gabe felt the storm of the season rolling in around him as he watched his mother follow the kids. Trudy looked back at them as she walked away; her troubled eyes connected with his and his unease grew.

"I have a right to meet my nephew."

Gabe wasn't a mean guy, just protecting what was his, but even he couldn't ignore the woman's confusion. "Look, I'm sorry I'm coming off so hard. But this is my son and I don't want him hurt. He's beginning to ask questions about his mother. Questions that tell me he's realizing there's a hole in his life where she's supposed to be."

"I don't see where that concerns me. What about your mother?"

"My mother is great. But he understands that she is his grandmother. The other boys have younger mothers. He's noticing. You're his aunt, and I just don't want to confuse him any more than he already is." Not to mention at some point Wes was going to also learn he had a sister. Gabe had only recently located Lilly but hadn't had a chance to make contact. And frankly, hadn't been sure if he should.

"I'm here to get to know him. Not to harm him. If that's what you're afraid of, you can relax. My sister was about his age the last time I ever saw her." She swallowed hard and blinked as if to ward off tears. "I just need to know him."

Oh, no…not tears. Gabe shifted uncomfortably, trying to figure out what to say or do.

She met and held his gaze straight on, all brightness that could be tears gone. "Don't get nervous, Gabe. I don't cry."

He locked his spine. "I wasn't nervous."

"Oh, yes you were. I saw terror in your eyes."

Terror. "I wasn't terrified."

She gave a husky chuckle. "Yes you were. But most men are terrified of crying women. So relax. Around me you're safe."

This was far more uncomfortable than she'd dreamed it would be. Olivia couldn't figure out why Gabe was so hostile about her being here. She was determined to make the best of it. She was determined to hold on to the joy she'd felt upon finding out about Wes. She followed Gabe down the hall of the spacious ranch house. He carried their large suitcases and led the way to her and Trudy's rooms. She couldn't help but wonder about the man her sister had fallen in love with. He seemed hard…but then, he was probably just feeling protective of Wes. After all, he didn't know her. Then again she knew she wasn't a threat unless he wasn't being a good father. She got the feeling, despite their differences, that Gabe McKennon was a great father.

She liked that. Justin had been a great father, too. He would have protected Trudy from anything he thought had potential to hurt her. Sadness filled her momentarily, as it always did when she thought about living life without Justin. It had been three years since he'd been killed in a boating accident, and she was making progress. She'd filled her life with all kinds of things to keep her busy. Homeschooling Trudy kept her fairly busy— but it wasn't enough to take up all the hours in a day. She'd begun volunteering every leftover spare moment to some sort of organization so she wouldn't feel the loneliness that tried to overtake her when she wasn't moving.

She was the head of the women's group, the secretary of her Sunday school department, a member of the landscape crew and the hospital auxiliary, a volunteer at the senior citizen center—and they were a busy, busy group. Anyone needed a volunteer, she was it! You name the organization, she was there.

She hated to admit it, but after clearing her calendar for the next few weeks and heading out here to Mule Hollow, she'd actually felt a sense of freedom. There still remained, even with the gruff cowboy so adamantly against her being here, a sense of relief for the break from responsibilities.

"Here they are. Take your pick," Gabe said, stepping into the second room he'd indicated. The rooms were neat, decorated in Southwestern décor like the rest of the house. The furniture was rustic, bold like the man in front of her. She had to admit that she could see why her sister would have been attracted to Gabe before she fell in love with him. The man was easy on the eyes. Not that she'd noticed that anymore. So many of her friends had tried to fix her up in the past two years. This year had been the worst. The busyness of her life had not only warded off the loneliness she felt, but it also gave her more excuses for not dating. Looking at Gabe, she couldn't help seeing the craziness of her situation. She volunteered to keep the loneliness at bay, and yet she had no desire to date someone to try and take that edge off. She wasn't going to say she would never remarry. She was only thirty…but she wasn't looking. She was searching for a connection to her sister right now.

"The house is wonderful," she said. "I love the décor. Did Dawn help decorate?" She didn't miss the flicker of anger in Gabe's eyes, and she almost wished she hadn't asked the question.

"Dawn wasn't here enough to decorate. This is what the place looked like when I married her. Look, I have work to get to. I obviously can't stop you from being around Wes since my mother set this ball rolling without consulting me. So I'm just going to have to trust you to take care."

Olivia started to tell him that she wouldn't dare do anything to hurt Wes, but Gabe didn't give her the chance. The man said his piece and then was gone. Turned on his boot heel and strode down the hall.

She stepped into the hallway and watched him march out the front door. His boots clomped on the porch as he went. The screen door slammed, and within seconds she heard his truck door slam, too.

Of all the rude, hardheaded men she'd ever encountered, Gabe McKennon topped the list!

Chapter Three

Gabe wasn't sure why he went to town instead of the pasture, where he could have been alone. Finding solitude probably would have been the smart thing. But his truck had turned left, and here he was, pulling up in front of Pete's Feed and Seed.

Like the rest of town, the feed store was a colorful sight. Bright yellow with green trim, it stood out almost—*almost*—as much as the outlandish pink hair salon across the street. If it wasn't for the array of colors, Mule Hollow would have resembled an Old West town the way it stood out on the horizon like a beacon. Of course, it was far brighter than any place he'd ever seen, each clapboard building painted a different color.

Wes was an old Western movie buff at the ripe old age of four. He'd asked Gabe if there were men with guns hiding up on the roofs the first time he saw the vividly painted town. Gabe smiled as he thought about Wes looking for outlaws on the rooftops. His son had an imagination and would hide behind the green picnic tables sitting on the plank sidewalks and pretend he was shooting the bad guys off the roofs.

Not today though.

Today Gabe was buying supplies by himself—nothing that really couldn't have waited. He'd just needed to get out of the house before he said something to either his mother or to Olivia Dancer that he might regret.

What had his mother been thinking? The question dug in like a thorn in his side, even now. When Dawn left the hospital and he'd had to bring Wes home by himself, his mother had never faltered. She'd left her life in the small town he'd grown up in and moved in with them. Recently, when he'd relocated to Mule Hollow, she'd moved right along with them. She'd been a lifesaver for him and Wes...

But she'd stepped over a boundary here.

She'd forgotten that Wes was his son, and if he hadn't wanted Dawn's family involved in Wes's life, then that was the way it should be.

But she'd given up so much for Wes and she

was, for all intents and purposes, his mother. She'd raised him right alongside Gabe. He wouldn't have been able to do it without her. So why was he so aggravated with her?

Because Dawn had been a piece of work like nothing he'd ever seen before nor wanted to see, or be involved with, again. The last person he wanted messing up his comfortable life was her sister. It didn't matter that they hadn't grown up around each other; Dawn's hurtful ways could have been genetic. It scared him to think there was a chance that Wes would take after his mother. It scared him to think there was nothing he could do to change the inevitable.

But he didn't like to think that way. Wes was sweet, kind and loving…and as open and honest as they came, even at his early age. Surely that would remain. One thing was certain—Gabe planned to do whatever it took to keep his influences positive. He'd thought Georgetta was on the same page with him on that, but apparently he'd been wrong.

"Yor shor mad at somethin'," Applegate Thornton said, striding out of the feed store, looking like he was on a mission. Gabe was used to seeing App down at Sam's diner, sitting with his buddy battling it out on the checkerboard. Even as aggravated as Gabe was, it struck him as funny that the dour man would ask him if he was mad "or somethin'."

"I've got something on my mind, App." App was hard of hearing so Gabe spoke loudly.

"It looks serious, that's for shor—it ain't nothin' bad about yor momma, is it?"

Well, it was, but he wasn't sharing that with App. If he did, the whole county might hear about it. "I just have an unexpected house-guest," he said instead. Everyone was going to know about Olivia and Trudy staying with them anyway.

"Yup, been wonderin' when she was gonna get here."

Gabe had been about to walk through the door into Pete's, but now he stopped practically midstep. "What did you say?"

A bushy brow shot up. "Yor houseguest. We been wonderin' when she was gonna show up."

Storm clouds had receded a little just by putting distance between him and what was going on at home. But now they rolled in over him again with a vengeance. "You knew I was having visitors?"

"Shor we did. The women been yabberin' about it down at the diner."

About him? About Olivia? How did they know about them? His mother had not only invited Olivia and Trudy to the house, but she'd been telling "the women" about it behind his back. He knew App was talking about the three older ladies in town—Norma Sue, Esther Mae and Adela.

"Why was my mother discussing Olivia with them?" He asked the question before his good sense could kick back into gear.

"Oh, believe me, they had plenty ta discuss. They ain't known as the matchmakin' posse because they don't talk. Or didn't ya know that? I forget you ain't been here all that long."

Gabe groaned. Surely not. "What exactly did they discuss *after* my mother joined them?"

Enjoying this far more than Gabe was, App grinned mischievously, yanked his thin shoulders back and drawled, "Well, Gabe, that ain't rocket science—they was discuss'n *you*."

"This is Duke." Wes sat down on the wooden steps on the side of the barn and tugged the cinnamon-splashed puppy into his arms. The dog was as tall as he was sitting down and filled his lap. He grinned over Duke's shoulder. "He's a doozy, ain't he!"

"Yes, he is." Olivia petted the puppy's head. "He looks like a good doozy though."

"Oh, he is."

Trudy was standing over near the pen, watching the horse in the stall. Wes scrambled out from beneath Duke and hurried to stand beside her. "You wanna pet him? Here, see." He reached inside the gate, and the horse instantly came to have his nose rubbed. "He likes it."

Trudy stepped close and hesitated, then reached and petted the horse's neck. Olivia smiled at the sight. Trudy loved books about horses, so this might be good for her, despite the fact that she hadn't wanted to leave her friends to come here.

"Would you like to grab a glass of tea and talk for a minute?" Georgetta asked as Wes began chattering away to Trudy.

"I think that would be wonderful." Olivia had been having fun getting to know Wes, but there was no denying that she needed to find out what was going on behind the scenes. "We're going up to the house, Trudy. Will you watch Wes?"

Trudy cut uncertain eyes her way but nodded reluctantly. Trudy had good moments and bad ones. This wasn't the best of moments, but it also wasn't the worst.

Olivia followed Georgetta back to the house

at a fast clip. Georgetta might be short, but she wasn't slow. In any sense of the word.

"Wes is a great little boy. My sister would have been very pleased."

Georgetta looked troubled. "One would hope she would be. But, I hate to say it—I honestly don't know what your sister would have felt."

This was too confusing. Olivia couldn't fathom the picture being insinuated about her sister. Or their attitudes.

"What do you want to know?"

"I need an explanation. Something to help me understand all of this."

Kind eyes met Olivia's and she braced herself for what she might hear in the next few minutes.

"Start with Gabe. What is so bad that he didn't want me here? Why did you tell me he knew I was coming when he didn't know?"

Georgetta stopped at the door of the house. "First, he'll get over being upset. He was wrong for not wanting you to come."

"Yes, I think he was. Still, this is going to be awkward. It might be better if I get a room at that bed-and-breakfast we discussed when you first called me."

"Oh, no, you will not! This is my home, too, and you are Wes's aunt. You'll stay here. Gabe is just, well, he's just concerned for Wes. He's afraid—" She halted and gave a caring smile. "He's afraid you might be like your sister. I'm sorry, that sounds horrible. Come on into the kitchen."

Her words shocked Olivia, but not so much today as they would have the day before.

"Have a seat. I'll get the tea." Georgetta indicated the large oak table in the corner.

It was a beautiful kitchen with tile floors and granite countertops. Bright sunshine glistened through the large windows. She could imagine lots of good meals shared by the family here in this kitchen. She was disappointed knowing that her sister hadn't helped with any of the decorating. Even more disturbed by the picture she was piecing together of her sister. What had been wrong with Dawn? How could she have walked out of the hospital and never held her son?

Georgetta looked sympathetic. "I guess you're realizing that things weren't great between your sister and Gabe." She set a glass of tea in front of Olivia and then sat across from her.

"It's pretty apparent."

"He was really hurt and angry... I take that back. I think he got over the hurt fairly early in the marriage. I don't know everything, just that things were wrong."

"Did she just get up and leave the hospital?" She still couldn't fathom such a thing.

Georgetta nodded, her eyes growing sad. "I couldn't believe it. I was there, and that day at the hospital when the baby was born, I realized things weren't right. I'd gotten the feeling when talking to Gabe on the phone, but he wasn't one to tell me much about his personal life. But when she left that next morning, took Lilly with her, it couldn't be denied. I'm sorry for you to hear these things, especially since Dawn is dead. I know my son is no saint, but it's safe to say Dawn had problems."

Olivia took a sip of tea, hoping to ease the tightness in her throat. "I can't understand all of this. I told Gabe that I hadn't seen my sister since she was about Wes's age. I've thought about her over the years so many times and wished I knew where she was. I prayed that both my sisters were safe and in good families like I was. God really blessed me with the beautiful family who adopted me. And then Maegan finding me was such an unexpected gift."

"I can't imagine what you went through being separated from your sisters. And you're a widow, too. You've had a hard life. But it seems you've been strong."

Olivia smiled. "God has given me strength. And I mean that from the bottom of my heart. My mom and dad were such great Christian witnesses to me. Still are." She didn't add that they had a little trouble letting go before her wedding, and then also after Justin's death. But she was fiercely independent and had become more so since losing Justin.

"I hope Gabe will relax. I'm sorry he's been hurt."

Georgetta reached across the table, laid her hand across Olivia's arm and squeezed. "My prayer is that this works out for the best for all of you. Maybe you are here to help heal some open wounds in my son's heart."

"Wait, I'm hoping that things ease between us for the good of Wes, but I don't know what I would do to help heal any wounds." She wasn't sure what exactly Georgetta was thinking, and she wasn't ready to lay all the blame for the bad marriage on her sister. From what she'd seen of Gabe so far, he was a rude, hardheaded man with the basic manners of an adolescent—and that wasn't being fair to adolescents.

For all she knew, her sister might have had a reason for her behavior. Not that Olivia could even begin to understand walking out on a child, but there could have been extenuating circumstances. And if there were, then while she was here Olivia planned to dig them out. And if at all possible, she would be able to see and share with Wes something good about his mother.

She hated to tell Georgetta, but she wasn't here to heal Gabe's heart; she was here for Wes. It was Wes's heart she was concerned with. *Not* Gabe McKennon's.

Chapter Four

"I think we've gotten off on the wrong foot," Olivia said, coming to meet Gabe when he got out of his truck. The woman didn't even give him time enough to set his boots on solid ground.

He tipped his hat back, his patience wearing thin. "I made myself clear when I talked to you on the phone. If there was any 'getting off on the wrong foot,' I'd say it didn't come from misunderstanding my wishes."

She bit her lip and stared at him. He got the feeling that biting her lip wasn't from indecision or worry, but more to keep her mouth shut. Clearly she would love to expound on her reasons for being here, but she was thinking it wasn't wise to do so.

"Oh, there you are," his mother said, poking

her head out the door. "Dinner is served. I'd begun to think you'd flown the country."

He was going to have to sit down at the table with her. The idea sent an uneasiness coursing through him. "If this wasn't my home, I might have thought about it."

Georgetta stepped out onto the porch. "Gabe McKennon, I'm ashamed of you."

"I think I'll go check on the children and wash up," Olivia said, not even glancing his way as she strode inside the house.

"I simply do not know what to do with you." His mother's exasperation rode shotgun as she glared at him. "I've taught you better than this. Yes, Dawn treated you badly, but that is no call for you to continue to behave in this manner. Up until this point I've been proud to call you my son, but this behavior is out of line and unacceptable."

He'd never had his mother tell him she was disappointed in him. Even though she had instigated this entire bad situation, the idea stung. "There is nothing good that can come of this."

"I believe there is a lot of good that can come out of it."

"I heard down at the diner that you've been holed up in the corner with Norma Sue and her bunch." He gave a warning hike of one of his brows. "I honest to goodness hope you haven't got some misguided notion that she and I would come near being a matchup. If you're stepping out on that limb, Mother, then we're going to have real trouble." His temperature escalated at the idea.

"Gabe. This is Dawn's long-lost sister. There is no danger here. She is a nice woman who happens to have lost her very dear husband whom she loved very much. Olivia is not her sister."

He didn't tell his mother that he had other things to worry about besides whether she acted like her sister. It was the mother instinct that had her coming all the way out here to find Wes that had him worried. If she found out his secret, he was convinced more than ever that she would try to gain custody of his son. Nowadays who knew what the courts would do in a situation like this? Fear like nothing he'd ever known gripped him even as he told himself he was being irrational. But when it came to his son, he was taking no chances.

"You coming in?" Georgetta asked, holding the door. "Wes had a great afternoon, if that relieves any of those stress lines etched about your eyes. He's crazy about Olivia."

He couldn't move as his mother let the door close behind her. What was she doing? Looking up at the blue May sky, he asked the Lord to give him some help. It wasn't as though he'd done a lot of asking for anything over the past couple of years. He hadn't wasted time praying for Dawn to come to her senses and return home. He'd seen the writing on the wall in her note. She'd used him with little remorse. He'd have been crazy to want her back after the way she'd behaved. Though he wouldn't have wished her dead—no, never that—but he had wished her to stay away.

Stalking up the steps, he took a deep breath and pulled open the door. Laughter burst out from the dining area, and Olivia's was unmistakable as it lifted above the others. The sound sent a shiver of awareness through him that took him by surprise, freezing him mid-step in the hallway. He didn't have to see the scene to know what he would find when he rounded that corner. It was the sound of laughter followed by teasing banter about Wes being a pint-sized cowboy…it was the sound of family.

It angered him that he thought of it that way. He had a family, and it didn't need to include a woman.

* * *

"Daddy, Daddy!" Wes shrieked, jumping from his chair to rush toward Gabe. He threw his arms around his dad's legs, who immediately picked him up and gave him a bear hug.

Olivia couldn't deny the hard tug at her heart as memories of Trudy doing the same thing to Justin hit the center of her heart. If she'd wondered at how loved her nephew was, she didn't have to wonder any longer. For all his difficult ways, Gabe loved his son and wasn't afraid to show it.

Burying his face in Wes's chest, Gabe sniffed. "You smell like a turtle."

"Is that good?" Wes giggled, squirming when Gabe tickled him. "I like um a lot."

"I don't have a problem with you smelling that way. Your grandmother is probably ready to get you into a bathtub as soon as dinner is over, though."

"How'd you know she done told me that?"

Gabe chuckled. "She was my momma long before she was your grandmother. She stuck me in plenty of soapy bathwater when I was your age."

"Oh, yeah. I forgot." Wes looked at Trudy. "Trudy don't smell like me. Why is that?"

Trudy looked indignant. "I'm not a boy. Girls don't smell."

At her daughter's words Olivia had to laugh. "Girls like to take baths more. That may be the answer."

Georgetta sat down beside Trudy. "Where Wes is concerned, everyone likes to take more baths than he does...but when Gabe was a boy, he was the same way."

Setting Wes down, Gabe mumbled something about washing his hands and then left the room. Olivia found herself wondering what he was thinking. He was a mixture of unrelenting brick wall and caring father. There was more in between the lines that made up the man, but it was these first apparent aspects of him that intrigued her. He was his child's protector, and for some unfathomable reason, he felt Wes needed protecting from her. This idea kept coming back to her. Georgetta had said he was afraid she might be like her sister. She wished she could understand that.

"Daddy smelled like a turtle, too." Wes's eyes were lit with admiration, as if smelling like a turtle was the ultimate.

"Me and you, kid," Gabe said, coming back into the room and pulling out his chair. He was sitting next to Wes and directly across the rectangular table from Olivia. He met her gaze with steady, unrelenting eyes. She got the gist—he and Wes were a team, locked together by an unbreakable bond. A bond that had far more than turtle smells connecting them.

"Gabe, will you say grace?"

Georgetta's question broke the tense moment. Gabe hesitated, then nodded, bowed his head and thanked the Lord for their meal. After a moment's hesitation he thanked Him for the people around the table and asked the Lord to bless them also. Olivia was certain he'd struggled with asking the Lord to bless her and Trudy when they were unwelcomed.

"Trudy don't want to get on a horse," Wes said the instant the prayer was over. He was looking seriously at his daddy. "I told her Pony Boy wouldn't hurt her. Tell her, Dad."

Olivia's heart tugged at Wes's concern for Trudy. He'd been trying to coax her onto that pretty blond horse all afternoon. Olivia knew in her heart that Trudy would love to get on the horse and ride. But she was reluctant to try. And since she didn't know how to ride, it would be dangerous.

"Pony Boy is gentle if you'd like to ride him. I wouldn't have a horse out there that could harm Wes or any other child." Gabe's expression was sincere as he placed a small portion of steak on Wes's plate, then passed the platter to her.

Olivia gave him a grateful smile for the way he was speaking to Trudy. He might be a hard man, but he had a soft spot where children were concerned. And he had no idea the sorrow that was built up inside her child. As much as she'd tried to get through to Trudy, the grief she held locked inside her was growing. They'd seen a counselor for a while but she hated it, so they'd stopped. Olivia prayed that she would deal with it when the time was right for her. Until then, Olivia just had to wait.

It hurt deeply knowing her child was in pain and she couldn't help her. But Olivia had dealt with Justin's loss in her own way and in her own time. It wasn't as if there was a timetable for grief.

"I just like looking at them." Trudy looked uncomfortable.

"And that's just fine." Georgetta patted Trudy's arm. "I'm not much on riding them, either. So tell us what kind of things you two do back home where you live."

Trudy toyed with her food, shrugged and remained quiet. Olivia felt the need to fill the silence. "We homeschool the first part of each day during the year. And then we keep busy."

"What do you do?" Wes asked, munching on his steak.

Olivia told about all the different organizations she worked with.

"If anyone needs a volunteer, my mom's the one to call," Trudy added drily.

Olivia gave her a smile. "You name it, I'm on it. No isn't in my vocabulary. Is it, Trudy?"

"Nope. When Dad was alive you didn't do so much."

"True." What did she say to that? When Justin was alive she wasn't lonely. There was a void in her life that was no longer filled. And truth of the matter was, it would never be filled again. It didn't matter if she volunteered for every committee twice and then some. But at least she wasn't sitting home in a dark room crying…no, not anymore anyway.

For some reason her gaze was drawn to Gabe's in that instant. He was watching her—though the moment their eyes met, he let his slide nonchalantly to his plate. But not before she felt a flutter of her pulse at the intensity of his gaze.

The feeling happened so suddenly she dropped her fork…and lost her mind at the same time!

Chapter Five

"Thanks for your help," Gabe called and waved as the four cowboys who'd helped him work cows drove away. The sun was beating down on him as he rode his horse across the pasture. Though the cattle he was taking to auction were now in the pen, ready to head out in the morning, he wanted to check on a weak spot in the fence he'd noticed earlier.

His mind, like it had done all day, immediately went back to the events of the day before. After dinner Gabe had excused himself and gone to his office to work. He'd stayed there until the house was quiet, and then he'd gone in to check on his sleeping son before he'd sneaked to his room like a thief in his own home.

How was he supposed to handle this? Not only the issues with Olivia, but there was

Trudy. It was clear the girl had some issues of her own. Anyone with eyes could tell that Trudy was having trouble, and he thought it stemmed from her dad's death. He could be totally wrong, but since he'd walked in her shoes, it was almost like looking in a mirror. He knew his mom had caught on early. There was no way she wouldn't have, as keen as she was in observing what bothered people. And there was Olivia. She was struggling, too—with all that going and joining she was doing there had to be a reason. Or maybe not. What was he doing thinking about it anyway? How many times over the last twenty-four hours had that question come up?

He was still asking himself the same thing later that evening after dinner. The woman was funny and bubbly, and his mother had been right…Wes was crazy about her.

After dinner he pretty much ran to the barn—he needed to feed Pony Boy, but he also needed some fresh air.

There was no way that he could be interested in the woman.

The idea hit him over dinner, and he couldn't shake it. This was the sister of Dawn. The woman he most needed to be leery of. The woman who very well could take the only thing in life that mattered from him. He was not interested in her.

Snatching the bucket from the nail in the feed room, he stormed out to the pens and scooped up a bucket full of sweet feed. Pony Boy nickered with enthusiasm. The horse was as old as Methuselah and that being the case he had to have extra feed just to keep weight on him. But the dear old horse was perfect for Wes to learn to ride because he was so gentle. One day when Wes was older he'd bring a younger horse around, but not before Wes was old enough to know exactly what he was doing. Horses were dangerous, and Trudy had every reason to be wary of them if she didn't know anything about them. He knew from experience that even the most knowledgeable could make mistakes. Caution was not something to take lightly where horses were concerned. His own dad had made a mistake and startled an injured mare when Gabe was ten. She'd kicked him with both feet and knocked him into the gate. He'd been dead before the ambulance had arrived. The memory and pain still affected him. He'd loved his dad like Wes loved him... Gabe's throat tightened at the thought.

"Are you angry about me still being here?" He swung around at the sound of the soft voice behind him. Olivia stood just inside the barn. The evening sun was setting behind her, and it made her look like she was illuminated in brilliant gold. Small dust particles played about her in the golden light. She made a beautiful image there, and he had to catch his breath. When had he been so affected by a woman? Not in a long, long time. He didn't like that it was this one getting to him after all this time.

"I guess you have a right to know your nephew."

She gave a small smile. "Thank you for realizing that."

Moving to the stall, he dumped the bucket of feed into the trough. His skin prickled with awareness when Olivia moved closer.

"He's fairly old, isn't he?"

"Yes. You know horses?"

She gave a small laugh. "Not that much. I just sensed he was an old soul when I was watching him yesterday."

Coming out of the stall, he closed the gate. Pony Boy stuck his nose over the gate, wanting attention. "He's a good horse." Gabe rubbed him between the eyes. "I wouldn't have him around if he was dangerous. If Trudy wants to ride, this would be the one."

Olivia moved to stand beside him, then

placed her hand just below his and rubbed the old horse's nose. He thought she was going to say something but remained silent instead.

She stood near enough for him to smell a light floral scent that drew him. He pulled back just before he leaned her direction and inhaled.

What are you doing?

"Your other sister—where is she?" He asked, saying the first thing that came to his mind. It had been four years since he'd been attracted to Dawn—and deceived by the power of that attraction. Looking at Olivia, his gut twisted, thinking how fickle he was. After all that Dawn had done to him, he couldn't fathom why looking at her sister, who resembled Dawn so closely, would draw him. It was as if he was a glutton for punishment.

Olivia pulled her hand away, turning toward him, her amber eyes troubled. "She went to find Dawn's other child, Lilly, and now she and Lilly's uncle are getting married. I still can't believe it. I mean, Maegan seemed so level-headed, and yet she meets this man— and before I can get my car gassed for the drive out here, she's engaged. I'm still a little troubled by that."

And with reason. Gabe frowned as red flags started waving on that one. His mother had said that just because they were sisters didn't mean they would be the same. He sidestepped, putting more space between him and Olivia. This revelation gave validity to his fear about bad family traits. "I'm glad to hear Lilly is doing good. I've worried about her."

"They're extremely happy, though, and Maegan called and can't wait for me to come visit. Of course, she has plans to come here and meet Wes, too."

"I'm sure my mother has already issued the invitation."

She crossed her arms and smiled. "Not that I'm aware of. I can understand some anger toward Dawn, but why do you dislike us so much? We've done nothing to you. We simply want to get to know our nephew and be a part of his life."

"And I'm seeing that I'll have to let that happen, to an extent. I already had located Lilly and planned for him to meet her."

"I'm glad for that," she said. "He enjoyed today. There was nothing wrong about today, except your behavior."

"That's your opinion."

Her brows dipped. "Gabe, I don't get you."

"Don't have to. If you'll excuse me, I need to finish my chores."

She stared hard, then, with a slight shake of her head, she walked away. He watched her round the corner and disappear. Only then did he breathe.

Two days down and nineteen more to go. It was going to be a long three weeks.

Olivia enjoyed the next three days. They were full of fun—when Gabe wasn't around. Georgetta took them into town and they ate lunch at Sam's, a quaint diner. They met several of the residents of Mule Hollow. The town was painted colorfully, and the people seemed just as colorful. There was Sam, the spunky owner, and the two hard-of-hearing checker players sitting at the front table of the diner. There was also a group of women around her age who were having fun eating lunch together when they arrived. She felt like they were women she would enjoy getting to know.

Still, tension filled the air when Gabe was around. At dinner each evening, she tried to ignore the fact that he was simply tolerating them. She refused to have his attitude ruin their visit, and so she kept her spirits up and made the time around the table together as fun and lively as possible.

Gabe might be counting the days until she

and Trudy climbed into their truck and headed back home. But Olivia couldn't worry about that too long. She had a little boy she'd fallen in love with, and she was having a wonderful time teasing, talking and playing with him.

Chapter Six

"So what do you think?" Norma Sue Jenkins asked with a robust smile.

Georgetta was joining her three friends for coffee because she needed their advice on how to help Gabe get past the anger he felt toward his ex-wife and move forward. She wasn't sure why she felt so strongly about it, but she had a good feeling about Olivia.

"I think she's wonderful. She's been raising her daughter ever since her young husband died, and though she hasn't said so, I can tell she is desperately lonely. She's involved with every kind of function and committee a person can get on. To me that means she's staving off loneliness. Filling her days with busywork."

"I agree," Esther Mae said. Her green eyes sparkled with possibility as she patted her freshly dyed red hair. "So how about sparks? Do you see any?"

Georgetta nodded. "Oh, there are those, but I'm not sure any of them come from a romantic idea. Although I've seen Gabe watching her even when he doesn't realize it. At least I don't think he does. He's so upset about her being here that I just can't tell. But wouldn't it be wonderful if they did fall in love—then Wes's aunt would get to help raise him, and Trudy would have my Gabe as a step-daddy. I think romantically, it fits wonderfully." She was wishing for too much, but it could work... couldn't it? "Gabe deserves so much more than he's had."

"Yes," Adela interjected. "But it has to be about the heart and God being in it. I've been praying ever since you told us Olivia was coming. I have a good feeling about this, too. If not for a romantic matchup, at least, I believe God is going to work in the situation for everyone's good. Especially the children."

Georgetta loved Adela. She was such a strong lady despite her very fragile look, with her porcelain skin and fine bones. "I believe so, too. So what do you ladies suggest I do?"

Norma Sue grinned. "Simple. They need as much time alone as possible. Your job is to figure out how to get it for them."

Georgetta prayed all the way home that she wasn't making a mistake pushing for Gabe and Olivia to get to know each other. She was worried, but really, she continued to tell herself, if it didn't work out, what could it hurt? It was better for her to try to help than to sit back and do nothing.

Wasn't it?

Trudy was sitting on a hay bale watching Pony Boy when Gabe walked into the barn. He felt for the kid. He wondered if Pony Boy saw the kid he saw. The one missing her dad so much it was written all over her for anyone to see. Olivia saw it; he was certain. He'd seen it in her eyes several times.

"I'd love it if you decided to let me teach you to ride him. He needs more exercise than Wes can give him, as young as Wes is."

She looked at him, not as startled by his approach as he'd thought she might be. Obviously her headphones weren't turned on, though the earpieces were planted in her ears. Slowly she pulled them out and let them drop around her shoulders. "I don't want to."

He shrugged. "That's fine." Walking over, he picked up a brush and opened the stall gate. "You want to help me brush him down?"

It was her turn to shrug. But she followed him inside and watched as he began brushing the horse's coat. "You know, I lost my dad when I was ten." He said the words carefully. Remembering as the feelings of loss beat heavy in his heart. "It hurts."

She walked closer. Her head bobbed. "Yeah, it does."

"Are you doing okay?" He wanted to hug her.

She looked at the ground and nodded.

His heart twisted tighter. "You want to brush?"

She pushed her long hair behind her ears and thought about it. She looked like her mother in a slight way but he was pretty positive, by the lighter color of her hair and the square, stubborn set to her jaw, that she looked more like her dad.

"Sure," she said at last.

He handed over the brush. "Have you ever groomed a horse before?"

"A few times at my friend's house. But it's been a while."

"Don't be nervous. Do just what I was doing,

using long strokes. It will get all the dirt off his coat and make him shine."

He watched as she worked. She seemed to relax. He wanted to ask if she needed to talk about anything. But he didn't. He'd told her they had common ground—sad but true—and he knew, like he had when he was her age, that she'd open up if she needed to.

"Does it always hurt?"

Her soft words touched him. "Yes. But the pain eases up after a bit."

She didn't look convinced but kept on working. "I like this horse."

"Good. Do you want to ride him?"

Trudy was riding Pony Boy! Olivia rounded the corner of the barn and almost tripped. Standing in the center of the riding pen, Gabe held the halter rope as Trudy rode the horse. Not wanting to disturb them but not wanting to miss out on her daughter on a horse, Olivia chose to watch from the shadows. Twenty minutes later Trudy climbed from the horse— and gave Gabe a hug.

It hit Olivia's heart hard and kicked her feet from beneath her. Weak in the knees, she hurried to the house, sank into the swing on the front porch and waited for Trudy to head inside. Her daughter needed a daddy.

The idea hurt. She'd had a daddy, and to consider replacing Justin was unthinkable. And yet—did God have someone out there to fill this void left inside of her and her child?

That remained to be seen, but Olivia knew it was a possibility she needed to open her heart to.

"Thank you."

Gabe's pulse hummed at the sound of Olivia's voice behind him. He'd been thinking about her a lot, and it bothered him that he found her so attractive. "For what?"

He tensed as she came to stand a few feet away from him. At supper she'd laughed and told stories of the older people she enjoyed working with at the senior citizens' home. She seemed to enjoy spending time there, and it didn't even have to be said that her being there was good for them. Just her smile alone lit up a room, but when she laughed…it bubbled out of her and made everything seem lighter. Even Trudy, as sullen as she could be, couldn't help but laugh at her mother talking about racing Mr. Blossom around the nurse's station in a wheelchair.

He'd been even more surprised when Trudy told him, while she was riding, that her mother had had twenty proposals of marriage last year alone from the men in the nursing home.

It was obvious that he may have made a mistake believing that she could be like her sister. Still, he couldn't be too careful. What if she knew that Wes wasn't actually his son? He knew rationally that the courts would look at him as Wes's dad. He was. But still, the idea bothered him.

"Thank you for doing what you did for Trudy. She told me she rode Pony Boy, but I have to admit that I stood in the shadows and watched her for a few minutes."

"She's a good kid. She did well."

"She said your dad died when you were her age."

He nodded. "It's a difficult time." They stared at each other for a long moment. He felt a pull between them, as if there was an elastic cord attaching them, drawing them closer.

"You are a curious man, Mr. McKennon. Very rude sometimes, but you have a big heart."

He didn't say anything but pulled the lid off the feed bin.

She came closer. "It's not going to work."

He gave her a sideways glance, wishing she'd go away. "What's not going to work?"

"You aren't running me off. And I no longer believe you are a curmudgeon."

"Maybe you should."

She shook her head. "I believe we need to learn to be friends. Or maybe friends is too strong a word for you to be comfortable with. Maybe we just need to learn to tolerate each other for Wes and Trudy's sake. They're first cousins, and it should be important to you that Wes have family. You love him, and I do believe that if you look past yourself, you'll see that. He is such a wonderful little boy."

"Yes, he is." He was trying to protect Wes—right? From what, though? This woman seemed to be truly good, by all appearances. But Dawn had deceived him, and so could her sister. Yet she was right. Trudy and Wes were cousins, and despite everything, he knew that he was wrong on this issue. Wes did need family. Looking at her, he wondered was it himself he was trying to protect from Olivia?

He offered her the feed bucket. "One bucketful of that," he said, watching as she took it from him. Her fingers touched his as he handed the bucket over, and her eyes widened ever so slightly at the contact. So she'd felt it, too. Why he'd done it, he wasn't sure, but he was drawn to her.

Despite not wanting to be.

"Thank you," she murmured, then dug the bucket into the vat of feed.

"Why are you so sure I'm not selfish?"

"Because you love your son too much."

"And how do you know that?"

Instead of answering him, she carried the bucket to the stall and dumped it. He watched from the gate, waiting.

"Are you telling me you don't?"

"No! Of course I love my son."

She came to stand in front of him. "See, there you go. I rest my case. Even though I'm not at all certain why you weren't saying that from the very beginning. Was it some sort of test?"

He propped a boot on the stall's lower rung. "Maybe. I wanted to see what you'd say. Find out how your mind works."

She chuckled. "Or if I have a mind."

"You do."

"Did my sister?"

Like a thunderous storm, his mood darkened. "If you're going to bring her into this conversation, then we're done. I've told you I don't want to talk about her."

"I never took you for a coward."

Anger flashed through him. "Look, lady, who died and made you the smart one?" The instant the words came out he regretted them. Olivia went white as a sheet before stalking from the stall.

"Aw, no," he muttered, looking up at the rafters as he raked his hand across the back of his neck. Knowing he had to fix this, he strode after her.

"Olivia." He caught her before she made it out of the barn. "I'm sorry." He reached and took her arm, hoping to halt her. She stopped but didn't turn around. "I'm an idiot," he said, sick about the whole thing. Her shoulders sagged as he pulled her around to face him. The moisture on her dark lashes made him feel even lower. "Honestly, I didn't mean that. It was unsympathetic."

"You were right, though. I'm not the smart one," she said softly. "He died. I'm just the survivor. Taking one day at a time."

"And I'm the selfish jerk." Not sure what to do, he did the only thing that felt right—he drew her into his arms, offering comfort even though she might not want it from the likes of him. She came despite herself and for a moment seemed to wilt against him. Her hair was soft against his chin, and she smelled of that same soft scent that he'd been unable to get off his mind. "Are you doing okay?" He felt clumsy and awkward. "I mean, have you made it through your husband's death okay? It sounds like the total wrong thing to ask. I know it was horribly hard on my mom when she lost my dad. It was callous of me to say such a thing when I've been so close to the fire."

She dragged in a long, shuddering breath and trembled in his arms. "Most of the time. I just get caught off guard sometimes. Like now. I'm sorry." Her words were muffled against his chest.

"Don't apologize." He tightened his hold, hearing the trace of pain in her words. He understood, though he didn't want to. He'd rather that Dawn's betrayal hadn't hurt. He'd rather that he hadn't fallen for her. But there it was. He wouldn't have married her if he hadn't cared…at least a little.

Olivia drew away, looking up at him. Her lashes were dark and fringed rich, amber eyes. He'd thought they were Dawn's eyes but now realized that they were lighter, and her lips were shaped much fuller with a tiny indent at the edge. Funny how she didn't really look as much like Dawn as he'd thought. "You look like you've made it. You're strong."

"I had to be." She blinked hard and turned her head to hide the tear that slipped from the edge of her eye.

He lifted his hand and gently touched her cheek, turning her back to look at him. "You loved him very much?"

Olivia nodded. "He was a good man, the best. Funny. Sweet. Strong. Ever my protector. A wonderful Christian man."

Gabe wondered suddenly what words someone who loved him would use to describe him. Funny and sweet certainly wouldn't make the cut. Strong might not even be used. Protector—he could fill that role and feel comfortable doing it. A Christian man. He was, but these past three years had changed him. He'd grown more distant from God than he'd ever been.

Looking at Olivia, he felt totally helpless as the tear ran slowly down her cheek. He brushed it away. "I'm sorry you lost him." He offered the only thing that felt right to say.

Blinking away the last of the dampness lingering on her lashes, her eyes searched his. "Thank you."

Time seemed to stop as he stood there. It was like everything came into focus looking into her eyes. It was as if he looked into twin pools and saw the future. *Crazy.*

He wanted to pull back but found himself stuck where he was, holding on to her. Drawn to her like nothing he'd ever felt before. His gaze dropped to her lips.

She stiffened in his arms, drawing his eyes back to hers, and they were as startled as his were. Propelled to action, they both stepped away from each other.

"I—I—" she stuttered, turning to go but walking the wrong way before turning back. "I have to go. I have to—" She froze a few steps away from him, and her words broke off as she turned around and met his eyes with her own beautiful uncertain ones.

He stepped back. "I, um, I'm sorry," he managed before stalking out the back of the barn into the pasture behind him. He didn't stop until he was at the edge of the stand of trees fifty yards from the barn. His head was drumming, and his heart was pounding like an angry bull out for revenge. He couldn't focus. What had he been thinking?

He'd wanted to kiss Olivia Dancer.

But it wasn't that thought that had him weak in the knees and on the run. He'd seen a life with her in her eyes. And it scared him.

Chapter Seven

She'd wanted to kiss him. Olivia was still shaken by this when she woke the next morning. Wanting to kiss him—and after he'd comforted her about Justin! How could she have spoken her husband's name and, almost in the same breath, been thinking of kissing another man?

The very thought confused her as she'd hurried out of the barn. Lying still in her bed, listening to the quietness of the house, she closed her eyes and immediately saw the sunset from the night before when she'd hurried to the back of the house to think. She'd stopped at the edge of the yard, her head, heart and stomach in turmoil as she watched the sun setting in the sky. It was a beautiful orange and pink mixture, brilliant with golden light. God was outdoing Himself with the sunset…but what was He doing with her heart?

Ugh! She flipped onto her stomach and yanked her pillow over her head. *What are you thinking, Olivia?* The best thing she could do was to remember that she was here for her sister's son. She was not here for...for...this! Whatever a person called it when they suddenly went off the deep end.

And now you're going to have to face him.

"It's about time y'all came in here ta eat together," Sam said Thursday night when they walked into the diner.

To Gabe's dismay, his mother had insisted they all go out for Sam's all-you-could-eat fish night. Reluctant didn't begin to describe Gabe as he drove them into town. Wes loved fish night, and though Gabe wanted to say no, he'd given in when Wes had begged to go. It was easy to see that Olivia didn't want to come, either, but she agreed.

Like two sparring partners in neutral corners, they squared off before getting into the truck. She was just as leery of him as he was of her. The idea didn't sit well with him.

"We're here now," he said, shaking Sam's hand with an iron grip to match the older man's.

"You sure are purdy," Stanley Orr said from

his seat at the front of the diner. "Anyone tell you you look like yor sister?"

Gabe wanted to tell Stanley to get back to playing checkers and mind his own business, but he and his buddy App were here eating catfish, not playing checkers. Still, he wished people wouldn't bring up Dawn. Especially in front of Wes.

"Yup, you do look like her some," Applegate grunted, grinning.

"Thank you," Olivia said. "Georgetta showed me some photos of Dawn, and I think she was beautiful. I'm nowhere near that."

"You most certainly are," Esther Mae piped up indignantly as she came over to welcome them. "You are beautiful."

Everyone else who gathered around them joined in on the praise. Gabe caught his mother watching him with interest, and he set his expression to neutral. Or so he thought, but the gleam in Georgetta's eyes hinted in a big way that she'd seen something of interest. "Y'all want to find a table?" he asked gruffly.

"I wanna sit in a booth." Wes grabbed Trudy's hand and led her off in the direction of the booths with his grandmother trailing them. It took a few more seconds of conversation before Gabe and Olivia could follow them. When they reached the booth, it was to find that Sam had brought a child's chair to the end of the booth for Wes. But it was the empty booth seat that had him sweating bullets. To his dismay, Georgetta and Trudy were sitting on one side of the booth, leaving the other one empty for him and Olivia. There was no way he could get out of sitting beside her without making a big deal out of it. He was stuck.

Olivia had been walking in front of him, weaving her way through the visiting crowd. Sam's on Thursday nights was more like a family gathering. Folks wandered about, socializing before settling down to their own tables to enjoy their fried fish. So, being taller, he spotted their predicament before she did. When she broke through the crowd and spotted the seating arrangement, Olivia stopped dead in her tracks, and he bumped into her.

"Sorry," he said.

She glared at him over her shoulder.

He didn't blame her. He was in exactly the same boat.

Sinking. And sinking fast.

"Don't you just love this place?" Georgetta said from across the table as Olivia and Gabe settled into the booth seat.

Olivia tried to seem undisturbed by being forced to sit beside Gabe. She hadn't expected this. Nor all the attention they'd drawn. Okay, so maybe she'd thought a smidge that they would draw attention. After all, Georgetta had said they were being asked about. But there was something else she'd seen in the eyes of Georgetta's friends, Norma Sue, Esther Mae and Adela. Speculation? Joy?

Something…something that said they knew *something* she didn't know? But *what?* Or was it just her imagination? After all, she'd been thinking about kissing Gabe.

And thinking about it a lot since yesterday.

"I do." Wes scrunched his little face up and looked thoughtful. "I been comin' here since I was knee-high to a grasshopper. I think that's what Mr. App told me. You heard him, Grandma. Is that what he said?"

"Yes, Wes, that's exactly what he said." Georgetta ruffled his hair affectionately. "That means you were really small."

"Was I a baby, Daddy?"

"You were," Gabe grunted.

Olivia was trying to ignore the way his leg was bouncing in a nervous manner, causing the bench to move. It shocked her that he was nervous. Or agitated. That was probably closer to the truth.

They managed to make it through the meal. Trudy was a bit sullen, Wes was excited and Georgetta was talkative. Olivia found out that Georgetta wanted to travel some day.

"How about you, Olivia? What are your plans?" Georgetta asked.

"My plans? Well, Trudy and I are keeping busy. Like I said before, we like to stay busy. Getting her through school and college is my goal."

"Have you ever thought of moving?"

What a funny question. "Not really. Trudy has her friends. The idea did cross my mind not long after Justin died. But that seemed unfair to my parents." She didn't say that they had had a hard time with her coming here. "I had to work at maintaining my independence after Justin's death. My dad, whom I love with all my heart, would have tried to run our lives." She smiled at Trudy. "Gramps means well, but he is pretty headstrong and thankfully, I developed some of his personality after being raised by him all those years. If not for that, he'd have been directing my every move—believing, of course, that he was doing what was best for us."

"So you think you developed traits from your adoptive parents?" Gabe asked, wiping his hands on his napkin and turning slightly to give her his attention. His knee touched hers as he did. She pulled away, despite the surge of attraction buzzing through her.

"Not think—I *know* I did. I'm too much like my dad for it to be a coincidence."

Gabe's brows flattened as he thought about her statement. "What about traits from your biological parents?"

"I really don't know. I was a little older than Wes when they were killed in a car accident, and I entered the foster care program. I can hardly remember them."

"I don't 'member my mommy."

Wes's statement took them all by surprise. He blinked innocently as only a young child can do. Olivia would have hugged him if she'd been able to, but Gabe was between them at the table. "I wish we could both know her."

Beside her Gabe tensed. Olivia wished she knew more about Dawn. The picture she'd pieced together hadn't grown better over the past week. She decided that when they got home, she might need to put aside this attraction she was letting sidetrack her from her goal and question Gabe. It was time for answers. There surely had to be something good about Dawn that he could share with her and with Wes. Wes needed to know about his mom.

"You want to be my mommy?" Wes's question rang out unexpectedly, startling everyone. Smiling broadly as if a light had just gone on in his little head, he continued, speaking loudly and enthusiastically. "You can be Trudy's mommy *and* my mommy too!"

Chapter Eight

It bothered Olivia over the next few days about Wes wanting a mother. Wanting *her* to be his mother. After he'd made the statement in Sam's, everyone at their table had grown silent for a minute, at a loss for words. It was a good thing Sam brought their food when he did, and they were able to dig in.

It wasn't for her to tell him that one day maybe he would have a new mother. Or to tell him that it wouldn't be her. She did tell him that she was his aunt. His mother's sister, she had to explain again. But he'd said she could be his momma if she wanted to. It was almost like it was a game to him. The sweet boy just smiled the whole time. One day he'd be old enough to understand.

She'd wanted to speak to Gabe in private, but when they got home Trudy asked her to play a board game with her, was insistent about it. In the restaurant Trudy had seemed bothered by Wes's declaration, and so Olivia couldn't pass up the chance to have some one-on-one time with her.

As it turned out, she didn't get to speak to Gabe until the following day. Especially since he disappeared soon after they arrived home. But on Friday, to her surprise, Georgetta took both kids with her to town to buy groceries. She'd also noticed that Trudy was getting a bit bored, and Georgetta wanted to show her Ranger, the larger town about seventy miles away.

Instead of Olivia being asked to go along as she'd expected, Georgetta suggested that it might be good for Trudy to spend time with Wes without her mother there. Olivia agreed, and so here she was. It was the perfect opportunity to speak to Gabe about Wes. She told herself that she was not looking forward to spending time alone with Gabe—that she just needed to discuss all these issues. Nope, it had absolutely nothing to do with wanting to be around him…

She was lying, and she knew it.

Gabe McKennon caused something inside of her to come alive that she hadn't felt in so very long. When he looked at her, she felt like a woman. Even when he scowled at her. And boy, was he ever doing plenty of that.

It was apparent that he was as disturbed by the attraction as she was…and she could tell he was attracted to her. A woman knew these things. Even a woman as rusty at this sort of thing as her.

But did he still believe she shouldn't be here?

The day was cool, and she was sitting on the porch swing when he drove up the drive and parked his big truck. Duke raced to meet him, and he bent to pet the pup as soon as his boots hit the gravel. Long, lean and dangerous—the description took her by surprise, but that was exactly what he appeared to her. If she'd always felt protected by Justin, she knew the woman who fell for Gabe would feel the same way.

Then again, if that was so, why had Dawn left? The question that had begun to plague Olivia was why would a woman in her right mind walk away from a man like him?

It was incomprehensible to her. But then, she still didn't know the facts. Could there have been something in the way Gabe treated her that made her leave?

But if so, then why leave her baby?

Oh, goodness. Her mind shut down, stopped

rolling, locked down as he strode up the walk toward her. Her breath stuck in her chest. He wore a thin film of dust over his T-shirt and jeans, and his boots were outfitted with spurs so they jingled as he walked. Her throat was as dry as parched sand as he came to a stop just outside the shade of the porch.

"Hi." He pulled his straw cowboy hat from his head and slapped it against his knee. He glanced around. "Where is everyone?"

Her pulse was threatening to send her into a blackout, it was so erratic. "They've gone to town." *Really, Olivia, get your head back on straight.*

"Mule Hollow?"

"Ranger. Your mother wanted to spend some time with them alone."

His brows dipped, and she knew he was thinking the exact same thing that had crossed her mind as she was sitting here. *Had they been set up?*

"Yes," she said, looking at him. "There is a very good chance that we were set up."

He hadn't expected her to say that. She hadn't expected to say it, but she was nervous. Her stomach was rolling with a thousand butterflies. She kept reminding herself that she had to talk to him about Wes needing to know about his mother. So why was she thinking about how nice it would be to get to spend some time with him on the porch swing? The very idea shocked her. But it was the truth.

It had been a long time since she'd sat on a porch swing and talked with a man…Justin, to be exact. They'd enjoyed their talks. Their time together.

Her heart stumbled as she realized again that in this moment, she was thinking only of Gabe's company.

"I'm going to go clean up," Gabe said, his scowl telling her that he didn't like the idea nearly as much as she did.

Ha. How about at all, she thought, as he stomped up the steps and entered the house. She was about to get up when he poked his head out the door.

"Don't go anywhere. We need to talk."

"Oh, okay," she said, feeling a smile spread though her. Twenty minutes later, when he reappeared, she was about as wound up as Wes after eating too much sugar.

"I feel better."

He looked freshly shaven and his dark hair curled at the edges, still damp. He'd pulled on an orange T-shirt and a pair of unstarched, worn jeans. He looked more approachable than he had the entire time she'd been here.

"I have a new shipment of cattle down in

a lower pasture, and I need to drive out and observe them. Would you want to ride? I can show you some of the place."

This was totally unexpected. "Sure. I'd love that." She'd meant to talk to him about Wes. She'd meant to talk to him about her sister but instead, a few minutes later, she found herself riding beside him in his truck. They were bouncing along over the pasture and through several gates into new pastures. It was beautiful, and there were ponds everywhere. And deer!

"Look at that," she gasped when the first group of five dashed for the cover of trees, springing over ground as they raced. "They're so graceful. Oh, there's more!" She laughed as another couple flew from the shadows, startled by the truck. "This is so great, Gabe. Wes is going to be a lucky boy growing up here."

He was relaxed as he drove with a hand draped over the steering wheel and glanced at her. "That's the reason I chose this property when I bought it. I want to give Wes the opportunity to grow up as a country boy. And a cowboy." He grinned.

"Always a cowboy," she teased.

"Is there anything else?"

"Of course not," she chuckled, feeling great. "But I guess that depends on who you ask."

He cocked a brow. "The ones that count will believe in cowboys."

Olivia couldn't look away from him. "Then I guess I count," she said, knowing that she did believe in cowboys. Or in Gabe McKennon anyway.

They reached the cattle, and Gabe pulled to a stop beneath the shade of a huge oak tree so he could observe the herd. His head was reeling with what Olivia had just said. Had she meant she believed in him? The idea sent a thrill racing through him—he wanted her to believe in him.

He wanted it in the worst of ways. The realization was startling.

"There are almost as many babies as there arc adults."

He chuckled. "This is a group of mommas and babies. So that's generally the case."

"I guess that wasn't the smartest thing to say."

"City girl," he teased, feeling more lighthearted than he had in a long time as she smiled.

Settling into her seat, she relaxed, propping her arm on the open window as she looked about the pasture. "I could get used to this, I think. You cowboys call this work, huh?"

She hiked a brow that made him smile. "This part is tough, I have to admit. But somebody has to do it."

"You're doing a fine job, too."

"Why thank you. I try."

Their eyes held for a minute. Gabe felt restless suddenly. "Do you want to get out?"

"Sure." She reached for the door as if she, too, needed out of the confines of the truck.

The thought sent a pleasing sense of right strumming through him. She'd walked a few feet from the truck and was watching the sun as it began lowering in the backdrop behind the cattle. He had to tamp down the want to walk up and put his arms around her. But the desire was almost overwhelming. What was this? He'd never felt so connected to someone in all of his life. Never.

"He needs to know about his mother, you know." Olivia locked her arms—he wished it was to keep her from wanting to reach for him. But that might have been wishing too much.

"I've been thinking about that since yesterday." He had this burning grudge against Dawn, and yet she was Wes's mother. "Maybe you're right after all."

"I know my sister hurt you—no, don't get all defensive," she said when he stiffened at her words. "I'm not here to take her side. I'm here to get to know who she was, and as a mother, I'm disappointed in her choices. But I can't help but wonder what made her that way. I can't understand that she left you with the baby you'd conceived together. As a mother especially. But Wes needs to know something of his mother. Surely you can give him something. Georgetta talks a little about her, telling him that his mother loved him. But there are no stories there—nothing for him to latch on to."

What would she say if she knew the truth? How would she look at things if she knew her sister had married him just to leave him to raise the baby she'd conceived with another man?

"That's just it—there isn't anything for him to latch on to because there isn't anything there. I barely knew her. The truth is, I fell for her like a fool. One minute I was single, and the next I was a married man expecting a baby. I knew her name but absolutely nothing about her past. Nothing."

Olivia looked stunned. "But why? That doesn't seem like you at all."

How could he explain it? "I fell in love, hard

and fast. Dawn was everything I thought I'd ever wanted in a woman. A wife. She turned on the charm, had the beauty and caught me, hook, line and sinker…and I do mean sinker. It wasn't long after the wedding that the illusion faded, and I realized I'd been duped."

"But what did she want?"

He'd said more than he should have. But there was no way he could tell her that she wanted a daddy and a home for her baby. And yet, looking at the disbelief and concern mixed up in Olivia's lovely face almost made him tell her to see if—if what? *What about your son?*

"I guess she thought she wanted a baby. She realized quickly that she didn't. And she didn't want a husband." He gave a gruff laugh. "That's when I realized I didn't know her at all. I'd married a pretty outer layer of a woman with a shallow core." He didn't know any other way to put it. And yet he'd been pretty shallow himself for not taking time to really get to know the woman inside that pretty exterior.

"How sad." Olivia halted, her breath sounding short. "I'd hoped to know my sister. I wonder if the way she was came from her past. You know, maybe never knowing us, her sisters. She was so young, she wouldn't have any remembrance of me and Maegan. Or maybe she did have a shadow of a memory, and she was searching for something elusive."

He could only stare at Olivia. She had chosen again to look at her sister with compassion. It was aggravating. "Do you always try to excuse people's behavior by diminishing the bad things they do? Or is it something you do only for family?"

Her eyes darkened with—what? Disgust? At him? Or was it pity? The latter made his temper surge. "Why are you looking at me that way?"

"You need to forgive her. I'll admit this is not what I'd wanted to learn about my little sister. But it's obvious there is nothing I can do for her now. But Gabe, you need to let it go. If you don't, it will be unhealthy for you and for Wes. You need to move on. God is pretty clear that holding on to bitterness can rot a man's soul. It'd be a pity for this bitterness you carry for my sister to rob you of future happiness. It's not hurting anyone but you. And Wes."

"I can handle it. I don't talk about her, so how's it hurting Wes?"

"Because he'll eventually feel the feelings you have for his mother. Even if he has no memory of her and no stories or anything to build a character sketch of her in his mind, he will see your reactions and build it from that. He'll know your feelings. You *need* to let her go."

He hadn't thought of that. Was it true?

"Wes's only hope of knowing anything about a mother is that you eventually remarry."

For a small increment of time, the idea of what life with Olivia would be like had hovered on the outer edge of his mind. He hadn't let it cross into the light, but he knew it had been there. In his deepest heart he knew there was substance to Olivia. There was a beautiful person inside her beautiful skin.

He shook his head, trying to shake the picture he was painting. It was dangerous. Meeting her soft gaze straight on, he inhaled sharply. "I was a fool once. That won't happen again."

"That's too bad. Marriage can be a beautiful thing when two people love each other. I was really blessed to have had the marriage I did. Justin…he was a truly loving and faithful husband."

He'd known even before she said so that she must have had a wonderful, strong marriage with her husband. It hit him that Justin also must have known how lucky he was to have her. Looking at her now, Gabe felt a stab of jealousy. Justin had been one lucky…no, that wasn't true—Justin had been one *blessed* man. He'd known in his short life what some men never knew—true love. It sounded sappy, but Gabe envied him.

Chapter Nine

Dear Lord, what is wrong with me? Olivia prayed. She hadn't been able to think of anything much except Gabe ever since they'd talked in the pasture three days ago. After he'd said he wouldn't remarry, her heart had hurt for him. She wanted him to know what it felt like to be loved. Truly loved. Her heart was heavy for Dawn, but she understood that there was nothing she could do for her sister except love her child for her. That was the easy part. It was the part about Gabe that had her not sleeping and watching the clock each day until he arrived home.

He'd changed since their talk, too. He'd seemed less guarded, and at the dinner table he no longer sat with a wall around him. He joked and teased them. It was easy to see by the sparkle in Georgetta's eyes that she was pleased. Olivia knew that the bitterness in Gabe's heart had had his mother worried, too. She wanted her son married and happy, and she knew as well as Olivia did that he needed to get rid of the ill feelings he was carting around with him before he could move on.

Olivia had begun to pray that he would do that. God was a big God, and she knew He could wipe the slate clean for Gabe if only he'd ask for forgiveness and show a little grace to the memory of Dawn. She prayed that God would use her to help him do this.

What confused her was how deeply she felt about it.

"We are so glad you came," Norma Sue belted out on Sunday morning as Olivia and Trudy entered the Mule Hollow Church of Faith with Gabe and his family.

"I'm glad to be here. Georgetta told me it was a wonderful church and that the pastor really was a man of faith."

"Oh, Chance Turner is that for certain. He's a man's kind of preacher…no beating around the bush with him. He's a cowboy, and you know cowboys—they tell it like it is."

Gabe chuckled at that. "I think I know a few cowgirls who do the same thing."

Norma Sue stuck her fists on her very well

rounded hips. "I'm glad you noticed. I would never want to be known any other way."

Olivia hadn't known the ranch woman long, but it was easy to see that with Norma Sue, you got exactly what you saw.

They moved into the church and were greeted by many people as they went to their seats. Somehow, when everyone moved into the pew to sit, she ended up sitting between Gabe and Trudy, with Wes and Georgetta sitting on the end.

The preacher's sermon was simple and easy to understand, and as sincere as any she'd heard. True, he was a cowboy, and she had to admit that she'd never heard a preacher ask, at the end of the service, for anyone who wasn't a member of the church to "saddle up" with them. Or that if one hadn't accepted the Lord as one's Savior, Pastor Turner wished they would say their piece, talk it over with the Lord, then accept the peace He offered through salvation. She liked the way he spoke. It was real and fit the community. The walls of the church might be traditional, but it was filled with cowboy after cowboy, and so it was fitting that the preacher was one, too.

What hit her the hardest was that his sermon was on grace. Several times during the service, Gabe glanced over at her. She wondered if he connected the sermon with his own life. Even wondering about this, she felt good sitting beside him. She'd missed worshiping with Justin, and for a long time after his death going to church had been hard. But slowly she'd grown used to sitting without him beside her. Looking at Gabe, she couldn't deny that it felt good.

"Are y'all staying for lunch?" Esther Mae called, hurrying over as soon as they walked out into the sunshine.

"We certainly are," Georgetta assured her. "I packed a cake and a roast in the car." She turned to Gabe. "Would you two mind getting that for me? I need to talk to Esther Mae."

"Sure, is that okay with you?" Gabe looked at Olivia.

"I'd love to go get that cake. My mouth has been watering for it ever since I saw it this morning." Georgetta must have gotten up at the crack of dawn to finish the coconut cake so early. She glanced over and saw Trudy talking with a couple of boys about her age. She was smiling, and that did Olivia's heart good.

"So, do you play volleyball?"

"I love it, actually. Why?"

They were walking across the parking lot and Gabe's elbow grazed hers. "Because you are looking at some volleyball-playing mani-acs back there. Norma Sue is like the general giving orders to her troops. And Esther Mae gets so excited that she'll run you over in a heartbeat."

"Sounds like my kind of game. Do you play?"

"When they drag me out there. I prefer to watch. It's better than a *Rocky* movie."

"That I have to see. And I guess, since I didn't bring a change of clothes, I'll be watching myself."

"We'll watch together—how's that?"

She nodded, watching him open the back door of the truck. She moved to take the cake, but instead of handing it to her, he just looked down at her. Her heart fluttered, and for a moment she thought he was thinking about kissing her! The idea sent a shiver down her spine, and her throat went dry as the desert. Her heart beat loudly. "So," she croaked. "I guess we better get back."

He nodded. "Yeah, we better." Looking a bit rattled himself, he finally reached for the cake and handed it to her. Their fingers touched in transition. She was amazed how such a small touch could send every nerve in her body spinning.

Nope. No volleyball for her. She wouldn't do anything but make a fool out of herself if she got out there. When her nerves were shot, she didn't tend to have too much eye-to-hand coordination. She'd just be fodder for *America's Funniest Home Videos* if she tried to play right now.

They had a great time in fellowship at church. And though she was too involved in the moment to dwell on her worry, she knew God was listening to her prayers because of the message on the power of grace. She hadn't been able to tell if it hit home with Gabe, but she prayed that it had. Surely if Jesus could pardon people—sinners that everyone on earth were—then Gabe had to find grace for Dawn. It was the only way for him to be free. It was the only way for him to love again.

And she realized she wanted him to love again.

She wanted it more than she could understand, and her heart ached thinking about it. The thought of leaving in a week was heavy on her heart. If she could leave knowing he was better, it would be easier.

Yes, that was where all of her reluctance to leave was coming from. Wasn't it?

* * *

Gabe unhooked the cattle trailer from his truck just as the sun was setting. From this barn in the back section of his ranch, he could see the very tip of the house above the trees. If the house didn't sit on a hill, he wouldn't be able to see it at all. He wondered what his family had done today while he was at the cattle sale.

It hit him that when he thought of family, he'd included Olivia and Trudy along with Wes and his mother. He went still at the dangerous, unexpected thought. He knew he was in trouble thinking that way.

Just the fact that the feeling had come out of nowhere hit home hard. It had been a little over two weeks since Olivia had arrived at his doorstep, but it seemed like so much longer. It was as if he'd known her for years.

Watching the sun set, Gabe's heart was heavy. She would be leaving soon. The thought had begun to eat at him. It made him agitated. But it was foolish on his part to feel this way. After all he'd been through with Dawn, he knew better than to let his emotions lead him. He knew better than to let his heart—he yanked up on that thought the second it kicked in. His *heart* wasn't getting into this.

His heart was going to stay locked away behind closed doors. Hadn't he learned anything from Dawn's betrayal?

But you didn't love Dawn. You only thought you did.

This was true. He'd known that almost from the beginning, and yet he'd locked his heart away from everyone but Wes.

Even his mother had had trouble getting through the barriers at times.

Olivia wasn't her sister. The thought kept knocking on the door, and he couldn't help thinking about the Bible verse where Jesus talked about knocking at the door...all anyone had to do to accept His grace and love and forgiveness was to let Jesus in.

"Why are you comparing Olivia to a Bible verse?" he growled as he stalked to his truck.

The sermon on Sunday had been on grace. That God gave people grace, and if they wanted to be Christians, they had to show that same grace to those around them.

That came to Dawn.

He wasn't sure if he could do it. But he knew that had to be why he was comparing Olivia and Jesus knocking on the door of his heart. They both wanted the same thing of him. They wanted him to pardon Dawn. They wanted him to forgive her and move on.

As he headed home, he struggled. He wasn't sure if he could do it. But he prayed God would lead him. And he knew, at least, that was a start.

"What's Mother's Day?" Wes asked on Wednesday afternoon. Gabe had come home early to let them ride, and Wes was sitting behind Trudy as she rode Pony Boy in a wide circle around Gabe. At his question, Trudy glanced at Olivia.

"It's next Sunday, isn't it, Mom?"

"It sure is."

"We made a card about it in Sunday School. But we're not 'sposed to tell y'all."

Gabe was standing in the center of the pen holding the lead rope as the horse walked about him in a circle. As Wes spoke, Gabe turned so that his gaze met hers.

They were like magnets that were drawn to each other but couldn't be. They'd been catching each other staring over the last few days. Each time, her heart stumbled and knotted. Oh, how she… Stop. She knew she was on dangerous ground. Crazy ground.

She'd only known him for two weeks. *Two weeks.*

"You give your mother a card to show her you love her," Trudy said. She enjoyed making homemade cards, and Olivia cherished each one. "Who did you make a card for?" There was an edge to her voice that caught Olivia's attention.

"I made a card for Grandma, but I want to make a card for Olivia."

"But—" Trudy stiffened in front of him.

Olivia's heart cried out at the sweet, frank way he said the words. She would have to tell Trudy not to be upset with him.

"We can make cards. That would be fun. Wouldn't it, Trudy?"

Her daughter cut stubborn, slightly jealous eyes toward her. Olivia gave her an imploring look, asking her to give the child some slack.

"It would be fun," she said at last. Wes's squeal of delight would have made any other horse but Pony Boy kick up and run, but the good old horse just kept right on plodding along. Duke, however, jumped to his feet from where he'd been napping. The big puppy looked up at his little buddy with expectant, bright eyes.

Olivia bent and petted him. "It's okay, boy. He's all right."

But was she?

The very idea of Wes wanting to make her a Mother's Day card had her heart pounding. How, oh, how was she going to leave behind the child she'd come to love so instantly?

When she looked up, her gaze locked on Gabe. She saw that he'd turned as the horse moved around, and his profile was exposed to her. Was it her imagination or did he look pale beneath his tan?

Goodness, the web that was woven about them.

If she would let herself—and she wasn't going to—but if she let herself, she knew she could love him.

She knew she could stay here with Trudy and make this a family…if she let her heart go and have free will.

But she couldn't do that. She had to hold tight to her heart, to her emotions. She had to.

Chapter Ten

Olivia's heart was sad at the thought that she and Trudy would be leaving on Mother's Day. When she'd come to visit, she hadn't even thought about it. But now it seemed like such an inappropriate day to leave.

"You like it?" Wes asked, proudly holding up the heart card he'd so carefully cut out. She'd helped him with the scissors, and Trudy had quietly helped him with the glue and with placing white cutout hearts on the larger heart.

Olivia ran her hand lovingly down Trudy's hair, patting her shoulder. "You did a great job helping Wes," she said, smiling at both children.

"Do you like my card?" Trudy asked.

"I love it. Thank you." The card Trudy made was beautiful with cutout flowers and hearts and colored words telling her she was the best mom ever. "You are the best daughter a mother could ask for, honey."

"Am I the best son?"

Wes's question reached inside and broke all Olivia's defenses down. "Yes, you are," she said, unable to say anything but what she felt. Oh, how she wanted to be his mother. How she wanted to fill that role left vacant by her sister.

What a mess she was in!

"Are you all right?"

Olivia stiffened at Gabe's question but continued to stare out into the night. She hadn't been able to sleep, and so she'd dressed and come outside. The sky was beautiful and clear with sparkling stars so bright they looked like diamonds on black velvet. If only her heart was as clear as the dark sky, she would be doing fine. "No. I'm not," she admitted truthfully.

Gabe came up behind her, and though he didn't touch her she could feel him. Every fiber of her being was alert to him.

"Olivia," he said, his voice gruff and questioning.

She crossed her arms tighter and held on. If

she didn't, she knew she would turn and reach for him. But he wasn't hers to reach for. She had no one to reach for. Not any longer.

Closing her eyes, she reminded herself to breathe, trying to calm the quaking of her spirit.

"Olivia," he said again, and her heart stilled as he gently laid his hands on her shoulders and turned her toward him. Time was standing still as her gaze met his. "I haven't been able to think about anything but you lately."

Gabe's eyes were fierce as he stepped close and wrapped his arms around her. Olivia's breath caught, and she couldn't move. She'd longed for this in her heart of hearts—the knowledge whispered through her as Gabe lowered his lips to hers.

She hadn't untwined her arms, as if holding them crossed could keep her heart from completely opening. But as he held her and kissed her, she found them open and wrapped around his waist of their own accord. Her arms had been empty since losing Justin. Until Gabe, she'd only longed to have him back, filling the void he'd left in her world. But now, Gabe was here and it was right. She kissed him with all of her emotion. And it hit her that only love could make this so right.

Only love could have her letting go of longing for Justin and opening her heart for a new future.

A future?

She pulled back abruptly as it hit her full force that she had no idea if a future was out there for her and Gabe.

"I—think we need to move apart." Her words were breathless, shaken. As shaken as her world. He moved back, raking both hands through his hair.

"I'm not sure how this happened," he said. "I can't seem to concentrate on anything except that you're leaving in a few days."

"Yes. I am."

His eyes darkened with emotion, his handsome face distraught. "I don't want you to go."

Such simple words. Such complicated words.

"I don't want to go." *I love you.* She wasn't even shocked knowing this. She loved him. But she didn't really know him...did she?

How could she love someone she'd only met two weeks ago? She'd fallen for Justin quickly, but they'd dated for a year before actually marrying. But she'd known within a few weeks that he was the man she wanted to spend her life with.

So why was she in such shock that she could love Gabe?

Moving away from him, she walked out into the yard. Fireflies hovered in the field, and she walked toward the fence that separated the yard from where they were twinkling in the dark.

"I haven't seen these much lately," she said when Gabe walked to stand beside her.

"There are more of them this year than I've seen in a long time."

She looked at him, and her stomach felt unsettled by all that was going through her head and heart. "You're a good man, Gabe. I haven't told you that, but I've watched you over the last two weeks, and though I wasn't sure what you were doing when I first arrived, I do now. You really were protecting Wes. I hope you see now that I'm not going to harm him."

"I know you would never harm him. You are nothing like his— Like your sister."

"You know you are going to have to forgive her like I said before."

He didn't answer that. Instead he reached and traced his finger along her jaw. "I've been praying about it. I'm not sure I can. But Olivia, I know there's a reason you came into my life. I told you I didn't know if I could ever remarry."

"I think your words were more along the lines of you would never be a fool again. Which saddens me to see that bitterness getting to you."

He stepped close again. "I could move forward with you. You are good for Wes. You could be the mother he'll never know. You can be that connection to her that is so important to you."

Not worded exactly as she would have liked it to be, but still, he was asking her to stay. "I couldn't stay unless there was more reason than being good for Wes. As crazy as it sounds, I've fallen in love with you in a couple of weeks. That scares me. But it's true." There—she'd said it. But her heart ached, and there was nothing about the sound of the words that was romantic. It sounded stiff and short. Layered over by his bitterness and what he'd just said. No. As much as she loved Wes, she couldn't stay just because of that. It wouldn't be fair to any of them.

"I need to go inside, now." She started to go, then turned back and gently kissed him on the lips. "I believe you are strong enough and faithful enough to let Dawn's memory rest in peace so that you may have peace in your heart. It's the only way—if you believe there is a future for us—that we could have one. It would have to be on the right foundation. You need to be free of this bitterness."

He didn't say anything as she headed toward the house. She'd fallen in love, but there was no joy in it. Opening the door, she slipped inside the quiet house and felt as if she were closing the door on any hope that they could have a life together.

What had she been thinking anyway?

The best thing for her was to leave as planned. She and Trudy had a life in Houston. Houston was where they belonged. Not here, in Mule Hollow. Not here with Wes and Gabe.

"Mom, I can't find Wes." Trudy came into the kitchen where Olivia and Georgetta were talking. Olivia had been trying to keep her emotions hidden from Georgetta, but it was hard. She was very observant. And hopeful.

"What do you mean?" Olivia asked, standing up.

"Where did he go?" Georgetta asked at the same time. They were all walking to the porch as they spoke.

Trudy looked upset. "We—we went outside to play and I—" She stopped talking. "He went to hide in one of his secret places, and I can't find him in any of them."

Olivia tried to hold down the worry that filled her and remain calm. "He's got to be around here somewhere. Come on, let's hurry up and go check his hiding places once more. Maybe he was hiding from you when you looked for him."

Trudy looked pensive. "Maybe."

Twenty minutes later they'd looked at all the places where he'd taken them. The trees behind the barn where he had a makeshift fort built. The hayloft. The bushes near the pump house and the mesquite trees out in the center of the pasture. They called his name and spread out, but he was nowhere to be found.

"We have to call Gabe," she and Georgetta said almost in unison when they didn't find him in the mesquite trees. "This is too far away from the house. If he's gone farther than this he could be lost."

"He knows better than to go off," Georgetta said, worry filling her voice. "Come on, let's go call."

"No, you go call. I'm going to keep looking." Olivia couldn't stand the thought of Wes being lost. Her heart was pounding, and her hands were shaking as she turned to go. Trudy didn't move.

"Mom," she said, drawing Olivia back. "I—I told him to get lost."

"What?" She turned to her daughter. "Honey, why did you do that?"

Trudy looked grief-stricken. "Because he was talking about you and how he wanted you to be his momma. I—" she looked down at the ground "—I told him you were my momma." The last word came on a whisper and then a wail. "I didn't mean it. I mean I didn't—"

"Oh, Trudy." Olivia wrapped her arms around Trudy and met Georgetta's alarmed but sympathetic eyes. "I'll always be your mother. I'm always going to be here for you." Oh, how she prayed that God would allow her daughter to get over this fear that gripped her. She knew it came from losing her dad, but how could Olivia help Trudy?

Trudy nodded against her shoulder. "We have to find Wes," she whimpered. "He's just a little kid."

"Okay then." Olivia leaned back and gripped Trudy by the shoulders. "You come with me. Georgetta, you go call Gabe—as late as it is, you probably need to call in some help."

Georgetta nodded. "I'll call in the troops.

Don't you worry. This place will be crawling with help within just a few minutes. More Mule Hollow folks than you can shake a stick at will come. We'll find Wes, don't you worry, Trudy honey."

Olivia could have kissed Georgetta for her gracious handling of her child. She only prayed that Wes would be found safe and sound.

"Come on, Momma. Let's go find Wes."

"First, let's take the time to pray. God knows where He is, and we need to pray that He'll keep him safe and lead us to him."

Her face solemn, Trudy blinked big blue eyes at her. "But will He really hear us? Sometimes…I wonder. Daddy—" Her words broke off.

"Oh, Trudy, God always hears us. Sometimes we don't understand the things that happen, but you must know that He cares for you. He is with you even in the bad times. He always hears you, but He knows the big picture. I know you prayed for your daddy. But it was his time to go be with the Lord. We won't ever understand it, but we have to accept it. That doesn't mean it isn't going to hurt."

Trudy nodded. "I feel bad. Because I was

mean to Wes and he lost his momma and I lost my daddy. I shouldn't have been mean."

Olivia hugged her again. "You are ten years old. That's not old enough to always do the right thing. I'm thirty-three and I don't often do the right thing. God understands."

They needed to go look for Wes. "Let's pray," she said, and then said a quick heartfelt prayer that God would keep Wes safe and lead them to him. And then, hand in hand, they went to look for him.

Chapter Eleven

In a cloud of dust and gravel, Gabe slid to a stop and was out of his truck almost before he had it in Park. His mother had been able to reach him on the phone, a miracle in itself since mobile phone coverage was so spotty around Mule Hollow. A price one paid for living in this part of the country, but still, a bad deal when an emergency arose. Thankfully, today his phone rang despite the fact that he was in an area notorious for no service. God and only God was responsible for that phone call going through.

Obviously her calls had made it through to others because there were several cowboys arriving behind him and some who had just gotten there. Sheriff Brady and Deputy Cantrell's vehicles were there, but the men were nowhere in sight, so he hoped they were already on the search. Georgetta hurried to meet him. It had been almost twenty minutes since she'd called him.

"He's still missing. Some of the men are already out looking—Brady and Zane are out there. And—" She blinked back tears, glancing around at all the others gathering around. "And all of these wonderful folks are here, too. Olivia and Trudy are out there also. I'm worried that they might get lost in the woods. They don't know this area."

Gabe looked around the group, an assortment of Mule Hollow folks, young and old. "We'll find them," he assured his mother just as App and Stanley drove up.

"Where was he last seen?" he asked as the two older men climbed from their truck. Even Sam hopped from the truck with them. They hurried up asking questions as they came looking for all the world, like men on a mission. It reminded him that these three men were veterans, and it made him prouder than ever to know them.

"What kin we do?" App boomed, moving through the small crowd with Stanley and Sam close behind.

"It's gonna be dark in an hour," Sam said, throwing his chest out and his shoulders back.

As small as he was, he looked far more agile than his age implied and ready to take on the world to find Wes.

"Yeah," Stanley agreed, looking at Georgetta and then at Gabe. "Time's a wastin'—let's get this show on the road. What do ya need us ta do?"

Georgetta nodded. "Thanks for coming, guys," she said. "I was just telling Gabe that we last saw Wes here in the yard. He and Trudy came outside and he—" Her words broke. "He ran off."

Something in the way she said the words had Gabe questioning the information. "What are you not telling me?"

"Well, poor Trudy. She's just a little girl and she was hurting. He told her he wanted Olivia to be his mother and Trudy got jealous. She's still dealing with separation issues after losing her daddy. She's so sorry now, but well, she told him to get lost. That Olivia was her mother." She glanced at everyone. "She's only ten and her mother is all she has. She's dealing with very heavy issues and hurts. The death of a loved one cuts deep, especially to a little girl. She's so sorry she hurt Wes. Y'all have to find my baby and bring him home safe. For his sake and our sake and that little girl's sake."

"We'll find him. Which way has everyone gone?"

After Georgetta told him the direction Olivia went, he coordinated which way everyone else should go. Many of the men had their horses with them, and some had their ATVs. He took his truck and a load of men and drove cross country to the woods where Olivia and Trudy were searching. This section of woods led farther back to rough country. Wes was only four; that area was way too far off for a little boy to get to. Wasn't it?

Wes had been told to never wander off. This stand of trees was as far as he'd ever been allowed to go. He was a little kid and scared to go off too far. No, Wes had his little hideouts, but they were within range. Surely, somewhere nearby, they would find him.

Surely. Gabe stalked into the woods flanked by rows of friends and fought feeling helpless. He prayed as he went, needing the strength that he knew God would give him.

He called Wes's name, and he could hear echoes coming through the woods as others did the same.

"Gabe!"

"Olivia, where are you?" Olivia's cry from up ahead relieved and scared him at the same time.

"Here," she called, coming into view through the shadows of the trees. Trudy raced toward him and threw herself into his arms. Tears streaked down her face.

"We c-can't find him," she cried. "He's not answering us and it's all m-my fault."

Olivia looked pale and shaken as she reached him. "We've been going in circles," she said in disgust. "I'm useless out here. Thank goodness all of you have arrived."

Holding Trudy close, he felt his heart crack open for the girl's pain. It hit him that Wes had lost his mother before he knew her, and though he longed for a mother, he hadn't known the loss that Trudy had experienced. He'd felt it losing his dad, but time had helped heal the wound. Trudy had loved and lost, and the scars of that loss were still fresh and etched in her life forever. He'd been there and lived it. From the start he'd felt connected to her pain, and he'd wanted to help. "We're going to find him, Trudy. We've got the whole town practically combing the ranch. You hang in there, little girl—we're going to find him. Even App and Stanley gave up checkers to come find him. And Sam—see them through the trees?" App's voice boomed like a sonic blast as he yelled for Wes, and the sound of it caused her to hiccup a small laugh through her tears.

Olivia looked as if she was about to fall apart, too. Holding open his free arm, she came to him and buried her face against his neck.

"We're going to find him," she said.

Her breath was warm against his skin, and Trudy's tears were hot against his shoulder. Two weeks earlier he'd tried to send these two away, and now all he wanted to do was calm their fears and find his son. All he wanted to do was bring them all together…and his world would be complete.

The thought echoed through him like the sound of so many calling Wes's name.

"Let's go find our boy."

Olivia took his hand, and Trudy jumped out of his arms and ran ahead calling Wes's name at the top of her lungs. The sun was setting and the shadows were growing.

"Soon it will be dark. What are we going to do?" Olivia asked when Trudy was out of hearing range.

"We'll keep on looking. As they hear about this, every man and woman will be here. If they can bring their horses or ATVs, they'll bring them."

"Okay," she said, relieved. "You live in a wonderful place."

"Yes, I've loved it from the start when we moved here." They were walking fast, and his heart was heavy. Yet he felt peace. "You could be a part of this. Olivia." He tightened his grip on her hand. "You could marry me."

Olivia stumbled, and he jumped in front of her to catch her. "Hang on, I've gotcha," he said, steadying her.

"Thanks," she gasped, looking up at him.

"Now's not the time to talk about this, but just so you know, that's how I feel. And I know that's how Wes feels."

She touched his face. "This is so complicated. We'll need to talk."

"We will." He glanced toward the trees down the incline where they were standing. "What is that?" he asked, seeing a shadow in the bushes.

"What?" Olivia asked, but he was already moving.

"Wes," he called. "Son." He made it to the bushes and pushed them aside and there, curled into a tight ball, was Wes, fast asleep. Tears stained his little cheeks and Gabe's heart broke, but relief and thanksgiving flooded in as he sank to his knees and scooped his son into his arms.

"I was scart," Wes said, from where he was snuggled up in his daddy's lap. The living room was crowded with everyone who'd helped look for him, though many of them had already gone home to be with their families. Olivia and Georgetta had been rushing around serving coffee and tea and cake. Leave it to Georgetta to whip up two cakes while she held her position at the house in case Wes had showed up there. Now they stood beside each other at the kitchen's edge and took in the scene before them. Gabe held Wes, and Trudy sat on the footstool beside them. Already, Olivia knew her daughter was better, but she knew she was going to send her back to counseling for a while. She was just going to have to find a good Christian counselor who could help Trudy understand the worries and fears that she'd been trying to cope with since Justin's death. Hopefully, this time she would be receptive to it. Olivia felt like she would be.

"I just was sittin' in the bushes b'cause I was afraid of them ole coyotes. But then I went to sleep and my daddy came and found me. Jesus told me he would."

Everyone laughed, but Wes looked at them like they were crazy for laughing. "He did," he said again. "He came and sat down beside me and told me it was going to be all right."

Olivia's eyes welled with tears as she met Georgetta's red-rimmed ones. God had been there for Wes, there was no doubt. When she looked back toward Wes, she found Gabe watching her. Her heart stumbled like her foot had on the vine that had just happened to be sticking up out of the ground in exactly the spot where Gabe would see his sleeping child. Like she was certain God had been in charge of them finding Wes, she was certain as she smiled at Gabe that God was in charge of what was happening between them. He smiled back and her heart was a total ball of mush.

How had this happened? She had never believed she could love someone other than her husband. Never believed that God would be so good as to give her love twice in one lifetime. But here she was, blessed beyond measure. She simply had to figure out what to do about it.

She'd said earlier, it was complicated, but she knew God was going to lead her…them. He would be faithful and true.

God would lead them right. She simply had to listen to what He had to say.

Gabe had asked her to marry him. Sure, it had been in the midst of crisis, but he'd asked. She knew that for him, that was an unbelievably huge step.

It was late when they got both kids in bed. Georgetta had gone to bed, too, and that left Gabe and Olivia in the living room alone. Taking her hand, he led her over to the couch and sank down with her in the crook of his arm. Weary, she rested her head on his shoulder.

"What a day. I'm glad it's come to an end." He rested his head against the top of hers and hugged her tighter. "I love you, Olivia."

Her heart began strumming. Holding his hand in her lap, she smoothed her fingers over his. "I love you, too, Gabe. But we still have issues."

"Nothing that can't be worked out. The kids will be great with us. Trudy is going to be fine. I know Wes is, too."

"I believe so. But I'm talking about our own issues. I don't know what drove my sister to act the way she did, but in my heart of hearts I know that you have to forgive her. I've said that so much, but it's what I know is right— I can't marry you—if that is really truly what you want—unless you find it in your heart to forgive my sister."

He'd stiffened against her, and she wanted to cry. Could he forgive Dawn? And if he couldn't, what was she going to do? Sitting up, she turned and looked into his dear eyes. There was such strength there. Such character. How had Dawn looked into these eyes and not fallen head over heels in love? How had she just walked away like that?

"I can't imagine how my sister could have treated you so badly. I can't fathom it myself. One look at you and I melt." She dabbed at a tear that sneaked up on her. "I feel so amazed that God has brought us together like this. I never thought, after Justin's death, that I would find someone else to love…and then I find you. And it's all happened so quickly. Too quickly. I'm almost afraid it's not true."

"You said you fell for Justin quickly."

"I did. I just can't believe it could happen like that again."

"You know a good thing when you see it." He grinned and she laughed.

"I didn't know you had a big head."

He turned her so that she was looking at him. "No big head here. I'm as amazed as you that I've found you and that I'm blessed enough that you love me. Olivia, we have a lot of plans to make and things to work out. But we can do it. After everything we've been through today and everything both of us have been through before, I know that we can do this."

"With God's help and blessing we can."

"With God's help and blessing." He repeated her words like a vow. "I love you and you're right, I have to let go of what Dawn did. I don't want any bitterness marring the life we can have together. I don't want Wes growing up and sensing that I feel anything negative about his mother. I've asked God to help me release the anger and to focus on what she gave me—Wes and also you and Trudy. How can I be angry at that?"

Olivia felt like she was in a dream. "I feel the same. Dawn led me to you, and I'll forever be blessed that she did."

Taking her face between his hands, Gabe kissed her forehead and then her lips. "I have to tell you something," he said, a few long moments later. His eyes shadowed. "You see, I didn't know it, but Dawn was pregnant with Wes when I married her."

"What?" Shock spilled over Olivia.

"I never knew until after he was born, and she left me a letter telling me that he wasn't mine."

Olivia couldn't believe it. "Wes isn't yours? Why would she do that?"

Gabe touched her lips with his fingertip. "Shh," he said softly. "Wes may not be my blood. But he is mine. I've loved him from the moment I first felt him inside his mother's womb. I've loved him from the first moment that I believed him to be conceived. I was afraid at first that if you found this out, you might challenge me for custody of him. But I couldn't marry you before revealing this to you."

She couldn't help herself. She threw herself at him and hugged him with all of her heart. "I knew I loved you for a reason." She leaned back and looked deeply into his eyes. "You, Gabe McKennon, are the most wonderful man."

He looked relieved. "I am the most blessed man if you tell me that you'll be my wife. That we can have a life together."

Olivia let all fear and worry go. There was no doubt in her mind that she was where she was supposed to be. "Yes. Yes, and double yes, I'll marry you." She laughed. "I can't wait to marry you."

Gabe hugged her tight and buried his face in the crook of her neck. She felt the tension ease from him, and she knew they were going to be all right. "Oh, Gabe. With God all things are possible, aren't they?"

"Yes. They are." He looked at her, smiling. "Do you want to go wake up everyone and break the news?"

Olivia smiled. Only a few hours earlier she would have been worried about Trudy, but now she felt Trudy was looking forward to this. "Yes. I would love to tell them."

Gabe stood, pulled her to her feet and kissed her so tenderly. And then, hand in hand, they went to wake up their family.

Epilogue

Six months later

"Run, Wes! Lilly is going to get you this time," Trudy yelled, laughing as his sister Lilly swung a rope over her head and tossed it toward him.

Wes was having a blast pretending to be a steer while his big sisters attempted to rope him. "Girls can't rope!" he called, as the rope landed beside him and Duke knocked him down and rolled on top of him.

Lilly and Trudy ran to his rescue. The girls had bonded immediately upon meeting, and both girls were crazy about Wes. Once Trudy had overcome her fear of losing Olivia, she'd been like a different child and loved the idea of having a little brother.

Watching them playing in the arena, Olivia

said a prayer of thanks to God for all of His blessings in their life. Things had been perfect since she and Gabe had fallen in love. But they'd understood that their love for each other had happened quickly, and they'd thought some time before the wedding would be good for everyone. They hadn't felt like there was a need to feel as if they'd rushed into anything and had decided to wait six months before getting married. Olivia and Trudy had gone home then relocated into a Mule Hollow apartment, and it had been such a sweet time for all of them to spend hanging out together and for Gabe and Olivia to actually date…or court, as App and Stanley down at the diner called it. Olivia liked the idea that they'd courted. She'd also liked the idea of helping Gabe get more comfortable with putting distance between the bitterness he'd felt for her sister and the forgiveness that he'd given Dawn so that he could move forward.

"Can you believe how our lives turned out?" Maegan asked, drawing her attention. They were standing beside each other on the porch.

Olivia smiled at her sister, enjoying the time they'd spent together for the last few days since the wedding. "It is still so hard to believe that after all these years we are together again. And that we are now the mothers of Dawn's children."

"God truly does work in mysterious ways," Maegan said softly, her voice filled with as much awe as Olivia's.

"I wish we'd been able to know Dawn— things might have been different for her if we could have all been together as a family." The ache in Olivia's heart for her younger sister would never go away. "I'll never know the answers to the many questions I have about the life she led after our parents died." It bothered her still, but she'd accepted there was nothing she could have done to change their past.

"We won't have those answers," Maegan agreed. "It is sad but true that we will never know if we could have helped her...but we know that we can help her children."

"Yes," Olivia said, reaching to squeeze Maegan's hand. "We will be the best mothers we can be for her children."

"Our children."

"Yes, we will," Olivia said, her voice cracking with emotion.

Maegan's gaze met hers in love and determination, two sisters locked together on a mission of love. Before they could say more,

Clint and Gabe walked out of the house, each coming to stand beside his wife. Maegan and her family were heading home to Colorado the next morning, and so the guys had cooked steaks on the grill, then helped Georgetta prepare the rest of the meal. They'd wanted Maegan and Olivia to spend time together before leaving.

"You okay?" Gabe asked. Concern etched his eyes as he spotted the emotion bright in Olivia's.

Clint asked the same of Maegan, who looked at Olivia once more and smiled as she nodded and hugged her husband.

One look at these strong, loving men of God, and Olivia and Maegan understood even more clearly how good the Lord had been in bringing them all together. His love was amazing.

They'd started out the aunts of their long-lost sister's children, but they'd ended up mothers.... God, as only He can do, and as He promises in the Bible, took their bad situation and gave it a wonderful, beautiful happy ending....

"We're fine," Maegan and Olivia said in unison.

"Just fine," Olivia repeated, kissing Gabe on the cheek as Wes, Lilly and Trudy came running up the path, their faces lit with smiles of joy. "Life doesn't get any better than this," she said, sweeping Wes into her arms.

"Better than what, Momma?" he asked. He was hot and sweaty and smelled like the back end of a cattle truck from playing in the arena dirt.

"Better than having all my family around me and you kids as a part of our lives."

"And me bein' your boy?" he asked, cocking his damp, dirt-streaked face to the side, his bright blue eyes beaming with love.

Olivia's heart swelled with love to match. "That's right, son. Having you as my boy is the best of it all."

He giggled at her words. "Even if I smell like a turtle?"

Everyone laughed.

Olivia hugged him tight, her heart so full of love. "Even," she said, "if you smell like a turtle."

* * * * *

Dear Reader,

Both of us (Debra and Janet) are happy to bring you another set of connected novellas. We see these books as special gifts to our readers (sort of two-for-ones), so we hope you have enjoyed these novellas the way you did the ones in our *Small-Town Brides* (published in the spring of 2009). This time we're celebrating family ties rather than brides, but the love is just as strong. Our heroines are sisters who were separated as children when their parents died, and they have only recently found each other again.

We know that some of our readers are in a similar situation and may not know the whereabouts of one or more of their family members (and maybe don't know where any of their family is). We hope our novellas ease that pain a little. Like our heroines, we know that God is with you and that He has a big family of fellow believers for you—they may not be your biological family, but they can love you just the same. You'll find them in churches, Bible study groups and Sunday school classes.

For the rest of our readers, we hope you

take a moment now and then to appreciate your family. Things may not always be easy between all of you, but God can work miracles of forgiveness and restoration. We pray He does, if that is what's needed in your life.

We both enjoy hearing from our readers so, if you get a chance, email us through our respective websites: reach Janet at www.janettronstad.com (use contact button on website) and Debra at: www.debraclopton@ymail.com or her website:debraclopton.com.

Sincerely yours,

Janet Tronstad & Debra Clopton

QUESTIONS FOR DISCUSSION

1. Olivia had a strong faith even though she'd been through some very hard times—her parents' death at a young age, being split up from her sisters and placed in foster care and the loss of her dear husband leaving her to raise her daughter on her own. Many people would blame God for the bad things that happen to them. What makes the difference between how people react to the blessings and the trials that happen to them?

2. Gabe was eaten up with bitterness at Olivia's sister. Olivia believed that this was bad for him and Wes's emotional well-being, and also for their future. Why? What do you think?

3. What does God say in the Bible about grace?

4. What did Olivia pray God would use her to do for Gabe?

5. The pastor's sermon was on grace. Grace is something we give even when the person or persons we are pardoning don't

deserve it. God gave us grace when He let His son Jesus die on the cross for our sins. Do you know someone you need to bestow grace upon?

6. Because he had lost his dad at an early age, Gabe realized that he could help Trudy deal with the grief she was still experiencing from the loss of her dad. Do you believe you can use your good and hard life experiences to help others? How?

LARGER-PRINT BOOKS!

**GET 2 FREE
LARGER-PRINT NOVELS
PLUS 2 FREE
MYSTERY GIFTS**

Love Inspired®

Larger-print novels are now available...

YES! Please send me 2 FREE LARGER-PRINT Love Inspired® novels and my 2 FREE mystery gifts (gifts are worth about $10). After receiving them, if I don't wish to receive any more books, I can return the shipping statement marked "cancel". If I don't cancel, I will receive 6 brand-new novels every month and be billed just $4.74 per book in the U.S. or $5.24 per book in Canada. That's a saving of at least 24% off the cover price. It's quite a bargain! Shipping and handling is just 50¢ per book in the U.S. and 75¢ per book in Canada.* I understand that accepting the 2 free books and gifts places me under no obligation to buy anything. I can always return a shipment and cancel at any time. Even if I never buy another book, the two free books and gifts are mine to keep forever.

122/322 IDN FC79

Name _____ (PLEASE PRINT) _____

Address _____ Apt. # _____

City _____ State/Prov. _____ Zip/Postal Code _____

Signature (if under 18, a parent or guardian must sign)

Mail to the **Reader Service:**
IN U.S.A.: P.O. Box 1867, Buffalo, NY 14240-1867
IN CANADA: P.O. Box 609, Fort Erie, Ontario L2A 5X3

Not valid to current subscribers to Love Inspired Larger-Print books.

**Are you a current subscriber to Love Inspired books
and want to receive the larger-print edition?
Call 1 800 873-8635 or visit www.ReaderService.com.**

* Terms and prices subject to change without notice. Prices do not include applicable taxes. Sales tax applicable in N.Y. Canadian residents will be charged applicable taxes. Offer not valid in Quebec. This offer is limited to one order per household. All orders subject to credit approval. Credit or debit balances in a customer's account(s) may be offset by any other outstanding balance owed by or to the customer. Please allow 4 to 6 weeks for delivery. Offer available while quantities last.

Your Privacy—The Reader Service is committed to protecting your privacy. Our Privacy Policy is available online at www.ReaderService.com or upon request from the Reader Service.

We make a portion of our mailing list available to reputable third parties that offer products we believe may interest you. If you prefer that we not exchange your name with third parties, or if you wish to clarify or modify your communication preferences, please visit us at www.ReaderService.com/consumerchoice or write to us at Reader Service Preference Service, P.O. Box 9062, Buffalo, NY 14269. Include your complete name and address.

Love Inspired SUSPENSE

RIVETING INSPIRATIONAL ROMANCE

Watch for our series of edge-
of-your-seat suspense novels.
These contemporary tales
of intrigue and romance
feature Christian characters
facing challenges to their faith...
and their lives!

AVAILABLE IN REGULAR
& LARGER-PRINT FORMATS

For exciting stories that reflect traditional values,
visit:
www.ReaderService.com